THE MYSTERY AT PEACOCK PLACE

Other **Apple** paperbacks
you will enjoy:

THE MYSTERY AT PEACOCK PLACE

M.F. Craig

AN
APPLE
PAPERBACK

SCHOLASTIC INC.
New York Toronto London Auckland Sydney

For Shadow
and his also remarkable people, Pat and Dick

ISBN 0-590-41174-8

12 11 10 9 8 7 6 5 4 3   9/8 0 1 2 3 4/9

Printed in the U.S.A.   28

CONTENTS

The Shattered Window

A stupid rabbit started the whole thing. There is no way that I, Hobie Morgan, or any boy in our town, would set a foot inside the Peacock Place on purpose. It is spooky enough when you ride past it on your bike and hear the coarse cries of those birds carried on the wind. The grown-ups shake their heads when they mention old Miss Peacock. They say she grew that hedge around her place and has Mr. Anderson run all her errands for her because she hates everybody in town. He manages everything at that place. She hasn't any family, except a brother off in Hong Kong or the East somewhere. Nobody I know has ever even seen her.

But we've all seen the Peacock horses. That family has been raising the fanciest Arabian horses in our part of the country for almost a hundred years. The Peacock horses, wearing fancy saddles decorated with the open fan of a peacock tail, have won blue ribbons all the way from our county fair to the American Royal Horse Show in Kansas City as long as I can remember. The star horse in the Peacock stable is a stallion named Caliph Haroun. He's worth a whole lot of money. Dad says that Miss Peacock has an insurance policy on Caliph Haroun in the six figures. That's a lot of money. He is a white horse with a coat so shiny that it glistens in the sun, almost as if it were reflecting the light like a mirror. All he has to do is prance by, to make any other horse look dowdy and ordinary. Even though Miss Peacock is supposed to hate everybody in town, nobody can say that she isn't generous with that horse. Every time there is a parade of any kind in our town, Caliph Haroun leads it off. The whole crowd starts cheering the minute they see those bright peacock colors flashing by.

A forest preserve runs alongside the Peacock property. It's hilly there, without too many rocks. I love to bike on that hill, pushing against the grade all the way up, and then bouncing down that uneven trail to the bottom. When your bike flies off a hillock and lands a foot or so beyond, it's really easy to imagine that you're not on a regular bike at all, but on a motorcycle, or a fancy dirt bike.

My friend Ben used to ride that hill with me all the time. I hoped that he would go biking with me that afternoon. I had even ridden out by his place to see if I could talk him into coming along with me.

I should have known better. Since last summer when we both turned twelve, Ben has spent all his spare time practicing drills for the Sheriff's Junior Mounted Posse, or going off with them to ride in parades.

That afternoon I found him out in the stable. Where else? He was grooming his horse, Tony. Ben spends as much time on Tony's looks as my sister Pat spends on hers.

"I'd really like to, Hobie," he told me. "But the Homecoming Parade is tomorrow."

"Really?" I asked him. I hate to be sarcastic like that, but Homecoming weekend isn't something that sneaks up on a fellow in our town.

He looked at me that funny way. "I get to carry the flag," he told me. He said it really carefully, trying to keep any sound of bragging out of his voice.

If I wanted to be honest with myself, Ben had every right to brag about that. You only get to carry the flag at the head of the whole mounted posse if you have trained your horse almost perfectly. An ordinary horse gets all excited and scared when unexpected things happen — flags can flap in a horse's face, sometimes a car backfires. The lead horse has to take all those things in stride.

3

I don't know whether it was disappointment because Ben wouldn't bike with me, or a little bit of envy over how good Ben was with that horse. Whatever it was, I felt mean. I didn't even tell him how great I thought it was that he and Tony got to carry the flag. In fact, I didn't say anything at all. I just picked up a stick and threw it for his dog and mine, who think they are puppies again every time they get together. The two dogs raced through the barnyard and barely braked in time to make it under the fence. Ben's dog Stormy beat my dog Shadow to the stick, but that was because he knew the territory better.

I just whistled for Shadow and said, "Well, okay. I'll see you around." Maybe I just imagined that Ben was sitting there watching me with a funny look on his face when I got on my bike and rode away.

Ben and I have been friends since the second grade. There are both good and bad things about having a friend that long. We've spent so much time together that we generally know what the other one is thinking. That's usually good. That afternoon it was bad because I was only thinking how much I missed his company, and I knew he was only thinking about that stupid horse of his.

I don't know for sure how it would have worked out if I had joined the Junior Posse when Ben did, but I hate to think I would be as cocky as he is about it.

Fortunately, my dog Shadow loves to run alongside when I'm biking the hills, so it's not as if I had to go biking all alone. Because of going clear over to Ben's farm it was pretty late when Shadow and I got out to the forest preserve.

We have a leash law in our town, so I always keep Shadow on his lead until we leave the road. Once we get inside the forest preserve, I take his collar off. It isn't fair for me to have all the fun.

Besides, I'm always afraid I might lose my balance and land on Shadow with my bike. He may be the greatest dog in the universe, but he only weighs fifteen pounds, which doesn't make him any mastiff. I've always been a pretty good biker, but I've grown so fast this last year that I've taken some real falls. Dad says he was awkward when he was my age, too. He says it's because your feet get too big for where you are going.

I had made three trips up and down the hill, with Shadow racing beside me, when the rabbit broke cover. It zigzagged in great flying leaps through the dead grass with Shadow right on its tail. I don't know how that dog can bark so loud and still have breath for running.

The rabbit must have gotten tired of being breathed on because it took a sudden hard right

5

and disappeared through the hedge that surrounds the Peacock Place.

Shadow is the kind of dog who minds you only when he wants to. Most of the time he obeys commands — heels when I want to show off, and even does tricks. But all the time we both know that he obeys only when he finds it convenient.

I had started yelling at him the minute that rabbit came flying out. I might as well have saved my breath because that's the kind of time that Shadow doesn't find obedience convenient. But it was one thing for him to chase that rabbit around the hill. It was a whole new problem for both the rabbit and Shadow to be on the wrong side of the Peacock hedge.

I yelled for him to come back and started after him. It was October, and nippy, so I was wearing jeans and a sweat shirt. A full suit of armor would have been handy when I hit that hedge. It's taller than I am, and made of some real boy-hating bushes with curly leaves, and thorns to match. The branches clawed at my face, and the thorns dug into my hands. Some of those thorns just jumped off their twigs and buried themselves in my jeans so they could keep on digging. Worse than that, the ground in under the hedge was piled deep with dead leaves — just the kind of rustling cover that snakes like best. With every single step I expected to come down on a rattlesnake and have it whipping around my ankles. Twelve is a very young age to die.

When I finally broke through the hedge on the other side, I fell flat on the grass. Shadow was nowhere to be seen, but I heard him barking wildly to the rear of the house beyond the stables. He must have chased the peacocks back there because they were screaming and squawking loud enough to drown out thunder.

I jumped to my feet and started that way around the house. It's the biggest house you ever saw, except on TV. The house itself is yellow, but it has millions of windows all trimmed with white, and crowned by curly, wooden ornaments. A little, black metal balcony runs around the very top of the house, with a forest of chimneys sprouting from the roof. Across the driveway in the front yard is a tiny little copy of the same kind of house, only open all around with vines climbing up the sides.

This sounds silly, but the scary thing was the silence of that place. Sure, I know that Shadow was barking and the peacocks were squawking, but all that noise fell into an almost eerie silence. You knew, you just knew, that if they stopped, the stillness would be so deep you'd fall into it.

I don't know much about horses because I don't care much about horses. That's one thing that my sister Pat and I have in common. Both of us had bad experiences with horses when we were pretty little, and have carefully avoided them since. But I paused a minute, wondering. The peacocks were making all that racket and Shadow was barking like crazy. It struck me right off that if there were horses behind the closed doors of those stalls they would be reacting in some way, kicking the walls or whinnying. Instead there was that silence.

The stables were painted yellow with white trim like the house. There were lights over each door, and a cinder path ran along in front where the stable hands led the horses out to exercise them, or load them into the horse van I always see at the state and county fairs. It is easy to pick that van out from the others because it has the fanned tail of a peacock painted on its side in full color.

At the end of the stable closest to the road was what looked like a big, long garage. Through the open doors I could see that it was empty in there, at least the first three spaces were.

I didn't realize how big peacocks were until I got to where Shadow had them all backed into the fence by the poultry yard. Some of them had jumped up on the fence, and were sticking their necks down to yell at him as if they thought he was deaf. I think he was glad to see me. Those birds really had him at a standoff. They kept darting those long necks down at him. While he wasn't about to get within reach of those beaks, he was too proud

8

to be chased away by anything wearing feathers.

When I called, Shadow turned and started toward me on his belly to apologize. He was licking his chops as if he could already taste the punishment he was going to get. Even after I put his collar on tighter than I like to fasten it, he still hung back, stiff-legged.

Finally, I picked him up and carried him. I knew he was scared worse than he let on, from the way he trembled under my arm. I wasn't too comfortable myself. There was something now about the silence that was more scary than the noise of those squawking birds. I had passed the house to go out by the drive that leads to the road when I looked back. The last glimmer of light from the sunset gleamed against the windows on the west side, but the ones in front were sort of in darkness, tall panes of blackness rimmed by white wood.

All but one.

I stopped and stared. A woman was standing in that window, waving her arms at me. With the light gone from the window you couldn't see all that well, but the woman standing there looked as white as a ghost; clothes, hair, and all. Even though I had never seen her, I just knew that must be Miss Peacock herself. I would have turned and run, having heard how she felt about the townspeople, if it hadn't been for the stick. As I stared, she grabbed what looked like a white stick

9

and smashed that window into a thousand pieces. The sound was musical, as fragments of glass tumbled down past the other windows to shower on the brick walk.

Then, as I watched, almost not believing what I had seen, she disappeared. She didn't go down or seem to step back. She simply disappeared. One minute she was there, and the next I saw only jagged edges of window glass, and blackness.

I have never been so scared in my whole life. You can't get to be twelve years old without learning that breaking window glass ranks right up there with treason. I took off down that gravel drive at some Olympic kind of speed. When I got to the gate, I shoved Shadow in under it first, then crawled out behind him.

I limped along for a few steps before even stopping to empty the gravel out of my sneakers. With Shadow still tight on his leash, I walked along the road, and up the field to where I had thrown my bike. When I lifted my bike I noticed that my wristwatch was missing. That made me really sick. My sister Pat had earned the money to give me that watch for my twelfth birthday. It was my first watch with a second hand.

Right away, I realized that it was too dark to find anything there without a flashlight. And I might have even lost it on the Peacock side of the hedge. I stared at that giant, thorny, green hedge as I walked my bike back down to the road. From the outside you would never dream what was in there — the giant house, the stables, and that eerie silence. Anything in the world could go on behind that hedge, and nobody would know it.

"I guess Miss Peacock really didn't want us in there," I told Shadow. "You have to want someone to get out of a place a lot, to break a window with a stick like that."

Shadow was panting, and wagging his tail in rhythm the way he does, and smiling.

"That will teach you to chase rabbits," I told him. He dropped his ears and tail, because my tone was so cross. I felt bad about that right away, and stopped to rub his head. It wasn't fair to take my anger out on him. I wasn't really mad at him at all. But I was pretty mad at myself for getting so spooked by that place, and losing my watch so that I didn't even know how late we were going to be getting home.

The Ivory Cane

All the way home I kept thinking about that window. Boy, you really have to be mad to smash a window like that, just because a kid is in your yard. Do you have any idea how much trouble a kid gets into for the windows he breaks just by accident? Just the idea that anyone could get mad enough to smash a big window like that was purely amazing to me. And I kept wondering if she really was mad. The longer I thought about the expression on her face, the more I thought that she hadn't looked mad at all, but terrified, as if she was scared out of her wits.

But what in the world was there for her to be afraid of? Even hidden away from the world as she was, she certainly must have heard that a kid and his dog amount to a less than deadly force.

I skidded into the yard and hit for the house in a hurry, hoping that Mrs. Kelley wouldn't notice how late I was. I was halfway glad Mom wasn't home, because she would notice for sure, and have a few well-chosen words to say about holding dinner for me.

To be honest, I'm not sure I would have told Mom and Dad about that little scene, even if they had been at home. Before I tell my folks things, I always try to predict what I'm going to hear back. That night I know I would have heard their standard lecture on other people's property rights. They might also have had some choice words to say about how much trouble a strongheaded dog like Shadow makes for everyone.

We were very sensitive about Shadow at our house right then. When Dad's plant was closed down, he looked everywhere for a new job. The closest work he had found was way off in Springfield. Our house had been on the market for months without being sold. Since nobody seemed to like it as much as we did, Mom and Dad were going to have to rent a house for us in Springfield.

Mom had gone there for the third weekend in a row to help Dad look for a house. There were plenty of houses for rent, but all of them belonged to really narrow-minded people.

"Two kids and a dog," they always said, and then started making rules that Mom and Dad knew we couldn't keep.

Mom had left early that Friday, and didn't plan to come back until late Sunday, unless they found a place.

When my sister Pat and I were little, Mrs. Kelley used to be our baby-sitter. But we're way past all that. Now Mom only has Mrs. Kelley in to take care of the house, and feed us.

The problem is that Mrs. Kelley has trouble remembering that we are practically grown-up. She still fusses about our drinking enough milk, and sleeping enough, and getting our teeth thoroughly clean. The worst is that she's always worried about our getting hurt.

The only way I had been able to talk Mrs. Kelley into letting me go out to bike at the forest preserve that late in the day was letting her believe that Ben was with me. I didn't exactly lie, I just gave her every opportunity to add two and two, and come up with eight.

The reason I have to go out of my way to fool Mrs. Kelley is that she is into horror. That woman can think of more dreadful things that could happen to a kid than you could see on a late, late movie.

Once I made the mistake of showing her an Indian arrowhead that my bike had kicked up from the dirt out in the forest preserve beside the Peacock Place. Right away, she started to worry about my being scalped. I had no more than talked her out of that than she remembered the little stream that runs through the forest preserve. Then I had to deal with her worrying about my drowning in one of those little five-inch pools, which are hardly deep enough to keep a tadpole wet on his back. Since it would be two more whole days before Mom got home, I wasn't about to tell Mrs. Kelley about going through that hedge into the Peacock Place. The last thing I wanted to do was spend the whole weekend inside the house looking out.

Don't misunderstand me, Mrs. Kelley is a really nice person, and I like her a lot, even though she is into horror and cooks funny.

She was making scalloped potatoes when I got home. She makes them the wrong way. She cooks the potatoes in watery little slices. Then she pours something thick and strange over them that makes them come out like hot library paste. When Mom makes scalloped potatoes, she rubs a big flat dish with garlic, and then butter. The potato slices are flat, and cook up crisp and brown on top, with Swiss cheese stringing with every bite.

I didn't dare stop to give Mrs. Kelley a cooking lesson. I was afraid she might notice how scratched up I was, and that I didn't have my watch anymore. I went right through the kitchen to find my sister Pat.

Pat is two years older than I. My hobby is doing tricks on my bike, hers is fooling around with her looks. I found her curled in front of the TV, painting her toenails a sickly shade of purple. Except for purple toenails, and pulling her hair all over to one side, and things like that, Pat is really pretty.

Even my friend Ben, who claims that girls make him sick, likes the way Pat looks. He says she has "good color for a chestnut." I'm not that good with the colors of horses, but Pat does have nice red hair that is darker than mine. We kid each other about our freckles. She says I have twice as many as I should, and I tell her she has half as many as she should. I'm almost as tall as she is, but skinnier in most places. She doesn't much like to be teased about that.

"Can you imagine anyone breaking the window in a house on purpose?" I asked her, needing to talk to somebody about what I had seen.

She frowned, and looked up at me with her head at an angle, the way Shadow does sometimes. "Maybe they lost their keys and needed to be inside in a hurry," she suggested. "Or fire," she went on brightly. "You're not really supposed to break a window in case of fire because it's dangerous to let all that oxygen in, but a lot of people do it anyway."

"This woman was upstairs shaking her hands at me and then she just smashed the window with a white stick as if she meant to throw it at me."

She straightened up and stared off into the corner, still frowning. Pat is the kind of person who likes to figure problems out and solve them. It makes her better in math than at being a sister, because she is always trying to tell me how to run my own life.

"Were you walking in her flower beds, or throwing rocks in her pool, or something like that?" Then she realized what I had said, and got really curious. "Who was it? Where were you?"

I pressed a finger on my mouth and nodded toward the kitchen where Mrs. Kelley was. "You have to promise not to tell."

I don't know whether it's that difference of two years between us, or just that Pat takes being the oldest child very seriously. In any case, she has a lot of trouble deciding whose side she is on, the grown-ups or the kids. She puzzled a minute before her curiosity finally won out. "I promise," she said. "Now tell."

Her eyes got really wide as I told her about Shadow going through that hedge, and my following him into the Peacock Place.

"That's it," she said. "Nobody is ever allowed inside there but Mr. Anderson, and the people he hires to work there. When Mom's garden club sponsored that house tour last spring, they wrote to Miss Peacock to ask if she would take part. There's a fortune in antiques in that house, and a lot of people would buy tickets to get inside that hedge. But the envelope came back with NO written on it. Nobody had even opened it to see what they were saying NO to. I'm really surprised that Mr. Anderson didn't drive you off. He looks cross to me."

"I didn't see him around anywhere," I told her. "In fact, it didn't feel as if anyone was there but her. And after she broke the window, she just disappeared."

Mrs. Kelley was calling us to come to supper. Pat held her fingers out flat, and screwed the lid on that purple nail polish without smudging a single finger. Then she swung to her feet, and looked at me with the sides of her mouth pulled down.

"Disappeared," she scoffed. "You mean she went away."

"She disappeared," I repeated stubbornly. "Just disappeared, that's what she did."

Pat filled our milk glasses while I arranged the chairs around the table. Mrs. Kelley was pouring bottled dressing on lettuce she had cut with a knife. Mom doesn't do either of those things. She makes her own dressing in the bottom of the bowl, with salt and garlic and fish paste, and vinegar and oil. Then she tears the lettuce with her fingers.

Mrs. Kelley kind of spreads out when she sits down. She did that, and then smiled at both of us. I really do like her, even if she is a strange cook.

"Did you have a nice bike ride, Hobie?" she asked me.

When I nodded, she smiled and went on. "I guess you didn't find any more of those Indian things."

"I wasn't looking for them today," I told her, wishing she would start asking Pat about *her* day.

"I've never really been inside that forest preserve," she mused. "But then I don't generally go out that way by the Peacock Place, since most of my friends live on the other side of town." She talked on, chewing thoughtfully. "Funny about Euphemia Peacock. Here all these years she has stayed locked up in that house. Now all of a sudden, she leaves on this big trip."

"What big trip?" I asked, almost dropping my fork.

She looked at me with as much surprise as I had felt at her words. "Why, it's all over town. I figured that everybody had heard it. Her brother is back in this country for a spell. He's staying out there taking care of the horses while she makes a long trip down to South Carolina. Mr. Anderson went along to drive for her."

"I guess I never even thought about her having a car," Pat said, fishing a cherry tomato from the salad with her fingers. "I only see Mr. Anderson in that horse van with the peacock tail painted on the side."

19

Mrs. Kelley nodded wisely. "That's the van he uses to haul the horses around for shows. But she must have a car. Why wouldn't she? With all that money of hers?"

I thought about that open door at the end of the stable. But the silence still didn't make any sense. Where were the horses that Miss Peacock's brother had come to take care of? The horses were always shown at the American Royal in the fall, but it couldn't be time yet, or Ben would have started talking about it. To hear him tell it, the American Royal is the single most important event of any year. Then, just like that, I could see that face again, white and terrified.

"Would you know Miss Peacock if you saw her?" I asked Mrs. Kelley.

I was clearly pinning her down too tight. She shrugged in a kind of angry way. "That lady is not interested in people knowing her. She's too proud by half, I'd say. She grew that big hedge up so that nobody could even see in. And that business with the birds. Peacocks, indeed! Wonder if the family name had been turkey? Would she have run turkeys all over that fine yard? They say she even carries an ivory cane with a peacock fan on the handle, something from her brother off in the Orient."

I looked up to see Pat staring steadily at me.

She was repeating something silently, making no sound at all.

"White cane," she was repeating. I could see her lips forming the words. "White cane. White, ivory cane."

Mrs. Kelley finally got around to asking Pat about her day, but I didn't even listen. Too many things didn't make sense. There was that business about the horses being absolutely silent with all that racket going on, and now this. If Miss Peacock was off to South Carolina, being driven around by Mr. Anderson, how could she also appear at that high window, and smash the glass with her ivory cane?

Homecoming

The next day was the Saturday of the annual Homecoming Parade and football game at our school. Homecoming is a really big event in our town. People who graduated from our school years before come back to see the game and to attend the Homecoming Dance that follows it. Mom and Dad had really tried to find a house for us earlier in the fall so they wouldn't have to be away that weekend. Homecoming was the one time of the year they got to see old friends who had moved a long way away and seldom came back. This was an especially bad year for them to miss it because Pat had been chosen as freshman attendant to the Homecoming Queen and would ride on the biggest float in the whole parade.

Dad likes the football game best, and Mom likes the dance, but the best part of the day as far as I am concerned is that big parade. Bands come from all the nearby towns; sometimes there are clowns, and there are always more floats than you can count. I had even worked on two of those floats. My Boy Scout troop had made one all in blue and gold, and my class made one with a huge whale on it. Andy Tripp was going to ride inside and push up a sign every once in a while that said, SAVE THE WHALES.

I had never missed a Homecoming Parade in my life that I could remember, but I had decided not to go watch this one. My friend Ben was going to carry the flag at the very front of the Sheriff's Junior Mounted Posse. I know it was mean of me, but I didn't want to see him riding by all high and mighty like that. Everybody knows that carrying the flag in a parade is the hardest position in the whole formation. If that flag flutters too much, or something spooks your horse, you can end up being bucked off right there in the middle of Main Street.

Maybe I didn't want to see my best friend made into a boy pancake right there in the street. Or maybe I was mad at myself for not joining the Junior Mounted Posse when I had a chance.

Ben had tried to get me to join back in the summer when he did. He showed me the special armbands they give you, and the saddle blanket in the posse colors, with the name sewn on just above the long, white fringe.

I told Ben I couldn't do it because I didn't have a horse. He said that was all right because his folks had extra horses and would let me ride one of theirs. Ben's family owns a farm out on the edge of town. They have four horses, and a pony that they keep for Ben's little sister. When I still said I didn't want to do it, he got mad and accused me of being afraid of horses.

If I had known that I wouldn't have any time at all with my best friend if I didn't join the posse, I might have forced myself to do it.

I'm not really afraid of horses. I think I'm just not ready for them yet. They're too big for me, and I don't like the way they stretch their necks around to look at you with their lips pulled back from those big, yellowed teeth. I also don't like how far their backs are from the ground. When I grow as tall as a horse is plenty soon enough to think about trying to ride one again.

Ben keeps forgetting that I haven't had the best luck with horses in my life. When I was about four, a friend of Pat's talked me into riding her Shetland pony. They set me on that thing, and put my feet in the stirrups. Right away it wasn't comfortable, because the pony was so fat my feet stuck straight out at the sides. Even so, everything went pretty well, until I steered the pony around so that he could see the barn.

That's when I found out that pony wasn't fat by any accident. The very sight of the barn made the pony think of his food, and how much he liked it. He started running straight for that barn. He only swerved from the beeline to try to scrape me off on the barbed wire fence on the way. By the time he finally got me off, I was so scratched up that it hurt to wear jeans all the rest of that summer.

But Pat's friend still wasn't satisfied. She told me the longer I put off riding again, the harder it would be. I finally agreed to try again if Pat would get up there with me. That time she put us on a full-sized horse.

Pat held the reins, and I held on to her. We just jogged along like a rocking chair for a few minutes, then the horse began to pick up speed. At that same moment, Pat started to yell at her friend that the reins felt funny.

"He has the bit in his teeth," her friend explained, running along after us, trying to catch the horse.

The horse ran faster than she did. He raced around the corral a couple of times with me hanging on to Pat, and bouncing up and down. Then he jumped the fence. The horse cleared the fence easily, but Pat and I didn't. Everybody took off trying to chase down that runaway horse, while Pat and I sat in the road trying to pick the gravel out of our faces and hands.

"You were right," Pat told me, when I finally

stopped squalling so I could hear her. "You were right, and I wish I had listened to you instead of her."

I especially remember her exact words because big sisters don't admit you're right that many times in a whole life.

The morning of Homecoming, Mrs. Kelley let Pat and me carry our cereal in by the TV. That way we could watch the Saturday morning cartoon until it was time for Pat to leave for the parade.

Pat was already dressed to ride on the queen's float. She looked funny in a party dress and makeup so early in the morning. She'd drawn a dark line around her eyes, and had painted her eyelids blue. She looked pretty enough in a magazine ad kind of way, but she didn't look like Pat.

We didn't talk until the commercial. Then she looked over at me. "You're not going to the parade in those jeans, are you?" she asked. "They have stains all over them."

I rubbed at my pants. "That's from the hedge I went through," I reminded her. "Anyway, I'm not going to the parade."

She stared at me, her eyes looking really big with those dark lines around them. Then she shrugged. "You could come to watch me even if you didn't want to see Ben."

"It's not Ben," I told her, even though that

wasn't the truth. "I just have better things to do."

She looked at me thoughtfully. "You're not going out there," she dropped her voice. "Out to Peacock's again, are you?"

When I shook my head she set her cereal bowl down very carefully. Her fingernails were painted that same purple as her toes, and she was frowning. "I know you must still be worrying about that woman behind the window. I kept thinking about her, too. What do you think, Hobie? What do you really think?"

I had seen Miss Peacock's face so many times in my mind that I blurted it right out.

"I think she is being held a prisoner out there, that's what I think. When I remember how her face looked, and the way she was gesturing with her hands, I think she looked more scared than mad. I think she might have been trying to signal to me, and somebody grabbed her away from that window fast so she couldn't yell for me to get help."

Pat straightened up and stared at the TV screen. Then she whistled out slowly, the way she does when she is thinking hard. "How could you get help for her?"

I shrugged. "I haven't been able to think of anything, except to go to the police, or to Sheriff Higher."

Her eyes were suddenly bright on mine. "What

27

a wonderful idea, Hobie. If you told Sheriff Higher exactly what happened and what you saw, he would go right out there and investigate it."

I nodded a little glumly. Pat hasn't had the run-ins with Sheriff Higher that I have.

"That's what you are going to do then," she said in this positive, eager way.

"I'm still thinking about it," I told her.

"Thinking about it?" She stared at me a minute before turning back to the TV screen. I could tell she wasn't seeing the picture at all. "Well," she said slowly, "if you *are* right, and Miss Peacock is being held a prisoner, you could be making it awfully dangerous for her. What if she is being held prisoner in there by someone who is stealing all her stuff? What if they plan to murder her when they are through?"

"Pat," I wailed. "Stop that."

"Stop that yourself," she said, standing up and looking down at me. "How would you feel if you were locked up someplace and the only person who knew you needed help was sitting on his hands? I sure don't envy the way you're going to feel when you find out that Miss Peacock has been murdered out there because you didn't do some simple little thing like talk to the sheriff."

No wonder she gets A's on her English papers. She's the only person in the world who could imagine a whole bloody murder and a lifetime of guilt from a broken window.

I heard her off in the kitchen rinsing her bowl and putting it into the dishwasher in a hasty, mad way. When she walked back through I pretended to be absorbed in a cartoon so I couldn't see her ignoring me.

In a way, I really was absorbed by that cartoon. It would be pretty marvelous to be some tubby little animal who could jump into a costume and have all the power in the world — just like that.

After Pat slammed out of the house, I went out back to see Shadow. He was lying half in and half out of his house. He lies there that way a lot, just staring. He has loose black, curly hair that springs up in all directions, and his eyebrows are about four inches long. When he lies like that, peering out from under the brush of hair, he's pretty comical. The minute he saw me at the door, he shot out of that doghouse to the end of his leash to greet me.

Shadow came from a litter of puppies that were abandoned out by Ben's farm. Ben has his brother, Stormy. They look alike, except that Stormy has a white mark like a saddle on his back.

Shadow was already a couple of years old before they passed the leash law in our town. That law has never been very convenient for him, but he seems to know that when I am in the yard with him, it's legal to let him run free.

The August before, when Dad and I had taken trash to the city dump in our station wagon, I found a big rusty hoop that Dad said had come from a barrel. Finding wonderful things at the dump is really easy. Talking Dad into letting me bring them home is something else again.

He did give in on that hoop when I explained how I could teach Shadow to jump through it. I tried hanging it on a tree limb, but it kept on turning. Finally, I nailed it to the top of one of Dad's sawhorses. If I hold a piece of liver cracker and coax and coax, I can get Shadow to jump through that hoop about one time in five.

"If he can do it once, he can do it every time," I told Dad, really annoyed at Shadow.

Dad grinned at me. "Is that right? Then why do you only get one spelling word right out of five?"

"The words are different."

"Every time you jump is a different one," he told me.

That morning when Shadow did two jumps out of five, I lay down on the ground and let him roll me around the way he likes to. I could hear that mixed-up sound that bands make when they are tuning up. Somebody with a drum was even drowning out the singing of the birds right there in the yard. I knew how it looked, with the band directors waving their arms this way and that, trying to get people together. Ben would be there with his horse and the flag, and Andy Tripp would be crouched down inside that whale with his sign.

Shadow sat still beside me, as if he was listening to the parade sounds, too. I shut my eyes and the parade went away. In its place was that woman's face, looking more scared than mad.

I rolled over and caught Shadow by the collar to put his leash back on. Mrs. Kelley was sweeping out the kitchen when I opened the back door and called in to tell her that I was going to the parade.

Shadow Again

My timing couldn't have been better. Just as I scooted through the alley to come out on Main Street, Caliph Haroun came around the corner, lifting those shiny hooves to flash in the sun. Deputy Ames, who was riding him, was grinning as broadly as Ben, who was following at the head of the Junior Posse carrying the American flag.

Something happens in my throat, making it thick and painful, when the American flag goes by. My eyes get watery, even when there's no dust in the air. And I'm really glad that I am a Boy Scout, so that I have an excuse to put my hand over my heart.

If a person could explode with joy, Ben would have been all over that street. Tony was lifting his heels as smartly as Caliph Haroun, and he was not batting an eye as that flag rippled and snapped around its staff. I wanted to poke the stranger next to me and say, "That's my best friend, Ben."

Instead, I just whistled and yelled, "That's the way, Ben!" as loud as I could.

He must have heard me because I saw him turn and look for me in the crowd. He didn't see me, but the look on his face stilled my voice. I realized with a start that I wasn't jealous of that horse of his, I was jealous of how happy Ben was, doing what he was doing. Fine friend I was, that I couldn't be glad he was having that much fun.

You couldn't stay unhappy, even with yourself, in that wonderful, noisy place. A couple of guys from my troop worked up to where I was hanging onto the lamp pole, and we all watched the parade together. I don't ever remember that many bands in a Homecoming Parade. Their uniforms were as many colors as the peacock fan on Caliph Haroun's saddle blanket, and the twirlers did things that I didn't believe with their decorated batons. A couple of clowns did handstands along the side of the parade, and a man wearing an Abraham Lincoln hat wove in and out between the bands on a unicycle.

You could tell when the Queen's float was coming, by the whistles and stamping. Somebody's little sister was standing up at the front throwing flower petals into the crowd. I felt one of them hit my face, but I didn't even brush it away. I was staring at my sister Pat as one of the guys elbowed my ribs painfully. "Wow," he said, "is your sister ever great!"

I only nodded. She didn't look like somebody I had eaten cereal with in front of the TV. She didn't look like anybody real at all. She looked like a movie star or something, wearing that crown of flowers with her head tilted at an angle like a dancer.

"Great," I murmured, thinking about her last words to me. "I sure don't envy the way you're going to feel when you find out that Miss Peacock has been murdered out there because you didn't do some simple little thing like talk to the sheriff."

I might have turned around and gone straight home right then, except that our class float was coming along. Andy Tripp came shooting up out of the whale to hold up his sign as it passed.

"Hey, Jonah," somebody shouted. As Andy went back down, he was giggling so broadly that you could see his braces shine in the sun.

The last float passed, and the crowd began to move away. A bunch of kids darted into the street, picking up streamers that had come off the floats along the way. I couldn't ever remember being so thirsty in my whole life. But even if I had thought to bring money, I couldn't have bought a cold drink. There was such a crush of people trying to get into the drugstore, that I had to wheel my bike past them in the street.

Anyway, I wanted to get back home. If I didn't see Sheriff Higher, it wouldn't be my fault that I hadn't talked to him.

I took shortcuts through the alleys because of the people walking home from the parade. I thought I made good time, but before I even got off my bike I saw Sheriff Higher's car turn into our driveway after me and stop.

The minute I saw it, I started getting mad. I just knew that Pat had decided that I was too awful to help Miss Peacock, and she had gone and told Sheriff Higher herself. He got out of his car and tugged his pants up the way he does, and waited for me to come over to him.

"Missed you at the parade, Hobie," he said.

"I was there," I told him.

"Nothing on your mind, is there Hobie?" he asked. The grown-ups are always saying how good Sheriff Higher is with kids. If they were kids they would know better. He's fair enough, but he has a way of making "good morning" sound like a threat.

My heart plunged. Pat really *had* told him. Worse than that, there was no telling what she had told him with that imagination of hers. "Never trust a woman with purple toenails," I told myself glumly.

I saw the curtain twitch at the window where Mrs. Kelley was peering out at us. Sheriff Higher must have noticed it, too, because he turned a little so that she couldn't see his face.

"Your folks down at Springfield house-hunting again this weekend?" he asked.

I nodded. "That's why Mrs. Kelley is there watching the house."

"Maybe she should be keeping a better watch on you, too," he said. "I got a complaint call about you down at the office this morning. Want to tell me about it?"

That time my stomach dropped all the way.

"What kind of a complaint?" I asked, hearing my voice turn high and quavery.

"You're not very convincing," he told me. "Maybe I ought to let you tell me all the possible complaints I could be getting?"

Since that wasn't the kind of question you could answer, I just waited.

"This particular complaint came from out at Peacock Place." He went on after a minute, "Mr. Peacock tells me that you were trespassing out there late yesterday, scaring those birds half to death."

"I didn't see any Mr. Peacock anywhere," I told him.

"He saw you," the sheriff said. "And he's not very happy with what went on, out there last night. Do you want to tell my your side of the story?"

"I was riding my bike up and down the trails in

36

the forest preserve," I began. "Then Shadow — "

He didn't even let me finish.

"Shadow, again!" he exploded. "Hobie Morgan, every single time you do something stupid, and get yourself in trouble, you blame it on that poor mutt of yours. This time you are really going too far. Don't try to tell me that a fifteen-pound dog dragged a big, husky kid like you through that thorn hedge of Peacock's."

I knew well enough what he was referring to. We both still remembered the time Shadow chased a cat across the railroad platform and into a boxcar just pulling out. Naturally, I jumped in after my dog. The cat must have shot right out the other side, but Shadow and I had to ride on to the next station. When the stationmaster took us off, he called Sheriff Higher to come bring us home.

And it really had been Shadow who had darted in under the flimsy legs of Mr. Zeffir's fruit stand that time, and turned Main Street into solid orange crush before they got the traffic stopped.

"A rabbit jumped and Shadow chased him through that hedge," I told him. "I went after him to bring him back out." I knew it sounded stubborn, but it was the honest truth.

"Now I guess you are going to tell me how Shadow managed to break that upstairs window," he said acidly.

I stared at him. "I didn't break that window. A woman with white hair, wearing a white dress, hit it with her cane and broke it."

He looked at me and laughed without smiling, which is an ugly thing to do. "A woman with white hair, in a white dress," he repeated slowly. "Of course you know that you are describing Miss Peacock. So you are telling me that a little old lady down in South Carolina slammed a cane through a window in Illinois?"

"Everybody may tell you that Miss Peacock is away on a trip," I told him. "But either Miss Peacock is there, or somebody dressed just like her is. Whoever was standing in that window had white hair, and a white dress, and a white cane. She stood behind the window making signs at me. Then she lifted that white cane and broke the window."

"So what did you do?" he asked.

"I ran," I admitted. "It scared me to see a window knocked out like that, and Shadow and I ran and crawled under the gate. I even lost my watch in there somewhere I was in so much of a hurry."

"And this was right before supper? Dusk like?"

I nodded. "But I could see her white hair and dress."

"You couldn't have been mistaken? You couldn't have just been holding a rock, and it flew out of your hand and hit the window?"

I shook my head. "I think she's being held a

prisoner there," I told him really fast. "I think she was trying to call out to me for help. When I couldn't hear, she broke the window and started yelling."

"Did you hear her yell for help?"

I had to shake my head again on that. "She didn't have time. The glass hadn't even stopped falling before she just disappeared from the window and it was all dark up there."

When a grown-up keeps on looking at you like that, just staring and looking as if every word you say sounds like a lie, you can't stop talking.

"What's more," I went on, "it's spooky out there. There wasn't any sign of a horse, and the big garage door was standing open. Maybe thieves have taken Miss Peacock prisoner and stolen all the horses."

His bellow of laughter interrupted me. "What an imagination you have, Hobie Morgan. If you saw the parade, you surely saw Caliph Haroun being ridden in full Peacock trappings by Deputy Ames, just as he always is. Ames had taken the horse to groom last night, because Mr. Anderson wasn't there to do it like he usually does."

That stopped me. "How did Mr. Peacock know it was me?" I asked.

That time the sheriff was grinning with his eyes, too. "Listen, when somebody tells me that a red-headed kid with a curly-haired black mutt does something, I am pretty sharp with clues. I admit I would feel better about all this if your folks were home, or if you would just tell me what prompted you to break that window. I've seen you do some pretty dumb things, but vandalism seems out of your line."

"The woman in white broke the window," I told him.

He shrugged. "Well, then it's going to end up with your word against his. And there's no way you are going to keep your folks out of this. I asked Mr. Peacock if he wanted to sue for damages. He said we could wait on that until his sister and Mr. Anderson get back from their southern trip. But you can be sure that you'll at least get a bill for the replacement of that window glass."

Somebody let Pat out of a car at the curb out in front. She came up the driveway smiling at me. I knew right off that she was proud of me because she thought I had been a good kid and talked to the sheriff. The sheriff grinned at her, too.

"The way you're going, Pat, you'll be as pretty as your mom someday."

Pat dimpled and thanked him, then ran up the front steps. She would have let herself into the house, except Mrs. Kelley had made it to the door and was staring out at us.

"Hobie and I were just gossiping about what a great parade this one was," the sheriff called to her. "Your grandson Ned did a great job on that bass drum."

Mrs. Kelley was grinning like a grandmother when she shut the door behind Pat.

"As for you, young man," the sheriff said, turning back to me, his voice threatening, "I'm not going to say anything to Mrs. Kelley because she flies off so easy. But you stay away from that place, hear me?"

I nodded. He started back toward his car, whose radio was chattering along quietly to itself. Then I couldn't stand it.

"Sheriff," I called after him. "Scout's honor she was at that window. She really was."

He gave me one of those looks and began backing his car out.

Second Thoughts

"**I** wish I had gone along to that parade with you," Mrs. Kelley said wistfully as I passed through the kitchen. "I would have dearly loved to have seen little Ned with his drum." She turned and smiled at me. "And your sister must have looked an angel. Are cheese sandwiches all right for lunch?"

This grandson that she calls "little Ned" is a senior this year. He is one of our school's best athletes and went to the all-state conference as shot-putter on our track team. Give the guy his due: Ned is a good shot-putter, and he beats a pretty mean drum. Little, Ned is not. I am a bit hazy about how many pounds there are in a ton, but I wouldn't want to go over a country bridge with Ned in the car.

"Pat looked great," I told Mrs. Kelley, too disturbed by Sheriff Higher's visit to give her cheese sandwich lessons. Every weekend that Mrs. Kelley takes care of the house she makes us cheese sandwiches for Saturday lunch. Every time I promise myself I will teach her how to make them right.

She butters the bread on both sides, puts cheese in the middle, and then browns the sandwich in the iron skillet. The right way is to spread a little Dijon mustard inside, put in the cheese, and then dip the whole sandwich in beaten egg and milk, as if you were making French toast. They puff up, and are moist and tart. You could eat five, if you had a belt that size. Maybe another Saturday.

Pat and I had choked down our sandwiches, and were enjoying the currant-pecan-oatmeal cookies that Mom had left, when the folks called from Springfield.

"I wish we had better news," Mom shouted, as if she didn't trust the phone wires all the way to Springfield. "But we haven't given up."

"Haven't you found anything?" Pat asked.

"Lots of nice houses," Mom told her, "but no landlord who will accept a dog. We haven't given up yet. Anything new there?"

"Not really," Pat told her, looking over at me as she spoke.

After promising to cheer the team to victory and be a good girl at the dance, Pat hung up. With Mrs. Kelley off into the other room, Pat leaned close to whisper to me.

"You are really wonderful, Hobie Morgan," she said.

I looked up startled, not realizing right away what she was talking about.

"I was afraid you wouldn't tell Sheriff Higher what you saw out at the Peacock Place last night," she said like a confession. "I underestimated you and I apologize."

I wanted to tell her right off what had happened, and how I didn't deserve any apology, but the phone was ringing again. Mrs. Kelley came and caught it just inside the door.

I didn't listen because I figured it was one of her children calling. But when she replaced the receiver, she folded back her sleeves to do the dishes and turned to me. "That was Sheriff Higher, Hobie." Her tone was so comfortable that I knew he hadn't told on me. All the same, I felt that cheese sandwich give a big lurch and start to pound itself around inside my stomach.

"You didn't tell me you lost your watch biking out there. The sheriff says he's planning to drive out by the preserve this afternoon, and will pick you up about four to take you out to look for it."

Pat and I looked at each other steadily. I knew she was thinking that the sheriff was taking me out to look for that poor, imprisoned woman. Sisterly pride simply shone on her face. I had no idea

44

why he was taking me, except that I didn't like it. Whatever glow I had was brotherly terror.

I have lived through some long afternoons in my life, but that was a world-class winner. By the time the sheriff finally pulled into our driveway, I was actually glad to see him. The cheese sandwich hadn't settled down, and neither had I. There was something to be said for getting things behind you.

"I'm not buying any more of your story than I did this morning," he told me right off. "But I did realize that I should have been watching that place closer. Generally my office keeps an eye on empty houses. I guess I didn't think about it because I knew Mr. Peacock was going to be there."

"Why are you taking me?" I asked.

"I thought a well-raised boy like you might want to apologize to Mr. Peacock for trespassing, and breaking that window. Also, bringing you out there gives me a chance to look around and see that things look okay." He chuckled. "You might even find your watch. I just mentioned that to keep Mrs. Kelley from ruffling her feathers."

When I didn't say anything, he turned his radio up and barked at one of his men who was patrolling the state highway just out of town. Then he turned back to me.

"Anyway, having a stranger like Peacock there is about the same as a house being empty. What does he know about this place after being gone from here for thirty years?"

I whistled softly. "Thirty years. You'll be lucky to recognize him."

The sheriff was turning into the drive that led to the Peacock Place. He glared at me. "What do you mean, recognize him? How old do you think I am anyway? Old Anderson is probably the only person around who would know him if he saw him. Now, get out and open that gate, you little bandit."

The peacocks were wandering around on the deep front lawn, feeding. They made the place look like a postcard. The minute that metal gate clanged, they began to screech and run toward the fowl yard behind the stable. They were making so much noise that my head felt as if someone was clapping his hands on both my ears.

As the peacocks ran screaming past the stables, a man stepped out to stare down the drive at us. The sheriff pulled on up toward the house, leaving me to walk. That was fine with me, I wasn't in any hurry to meet this man who had told such a crazy lie about me anyway.

The house looked just as it had the day before,

except for a piece of brownish paper or cardboard that had been fitted into the broken window. The silence was there, that heavy waiting kind of silence that made the yard seem cold, even with the watery, late afternoon sunshine casting shadows on the porch and along the cinder walk by the stable.

I saw the two men shake hands, talk a minute, then turn to watch me approach. The man waiting by Sheriff Higher seemed too young to be Miss Peacock's brother. I'm not really good at guessing the ages of grown-ups, but he didn't even look old to me. He was lean and muscular, built like a football player, heavy in the shoulders and narrow-hipped. His hair was dark, without any streaks of gray that I could see. But his face was deeply tanned, making his eyes look brighter than any blue eyes I had ever seen before. He must have been doing some kind of work around the stable because he was rolling his shirt sleeves back down as I walked up.

I know it was rude to stare like that, but I had never seen a real tattoo that big before. One of the men at Dad's plant had an anchor and the name Marge on his left hand, but this was a bunch of snakes all twisted up, with a hooded cobra's head coming out at the top and glaring right at you with bright, beady eyes.

"Hobie." Sheriff Higher's voice sounded annoyed. "This is Mr. Peacock, who reported your trespassing here yesterday."

The man stared at me wordlessly, watching me with those strange eyes. I could feel his cobra watching me through the cotton of the shirt.

"Well, Hobie," the sheriff prompted.

"I am sorry I trespassed," I said. "I came after my dog, Shadow."

"Hobie," the sheriff's tone had turned warning.

"I am really sorry I trespassed," I repeated.

"What about the window?" the sheriff asked.

The inside of my stomach had clamped around that awful cheese sandwich like a fist, but telling a lie wasn't going to make it any better.

"I'm sorry the window was broken," I said.

"Mr. Peacock saw you break the window," the sheriff reminded me.

When I didn't say anything, the man with the tattoo twisted his body angrily and said, "What do you expect out of a rotten little vandal?"

The sheriff was caught off guard by this. He cleared his throat, frowned, and said. "Go look for your watch, Hobie. I'll wait here with Mr. Peacock."

I tried to remember exactly where I had been in the yard. Because I could feel that man watching me, I decided to go toward the hedge, where

I had come in first, because it was the farthest place away from him.

I retraced my path from the house to the hedge a step at a time, looking down into the grass as I went. The men were talking and their words rumbled to me in snatches. I probably wouldn't have paid any attention to what they said if Mr. Peacock hadn't raised his voice in reply to Sheriff Higher's comment.

"They tell me at the courthouse that you attempted to have your sister declared incompetent about six months ago."

"My sister is crazy," Mr. Peacock said angrily. "I can't see how that court could decide otherwise. When was the last time she left this place? Only a crazy person would bury herself out here like she does."

I hadn't ever really seen Miss Peacock, except that shadowy way beyond the window, but his tone made me sick. What kind of man would have his sister put away as insane when she wasn't bothering anybody? More than anything I wanted to find my watch and get out of there, and never see his face or that coiled cobra again.

I was sure glad that I hadn't changed my jeans. I hadn't taken a step into that hedge before those thorns started to nail me again. But at the third step I saw something glitter in the bush at my

49

left. My watch was dangling there unfastened. If it had dropped down into the dry leaves I might have lost it forever.

The watch was still ticking. I fastened it on and turned to go back to the sheriff. Just as I emerged from the hedge, I looked up at the house again. The windows were all dark on this side, but at one of them something light was moving back and forth, as if it was waving in the wind.

I stared hard. It was a face, the same white face framed by pale hair. But this time I couldn't see a mouth. There was no darkness on that face at all, except the eyes, but she was wavering back and forth. She didn't raise her hands, just rocked back and forth like one of those toy clowns with the heavy bottoms that a kid plays with in a play-pen.

I was gazing at that moving face, trying to make some sense of it, when I felt Mr. Peacock staring at me. His look of hatred made my breath come short. Sheriff Higher turned, too, and asked, "You okay, Hobie?"

I wanted to tell Sheriff Higher what I had just seen. I wanted to cry out for him to help her. But he hadn't believed me before, and he wasn't apt to now. Anyway, he wouldn't believe me enough to make Mr. Peacock let him in, and go up there and look.

My voice sounded funny even to me. "I found

it," I told him. "I found my watch in the hedge."

"All right," Sheriff Higher said heartily. Then he turned and shook Mr. Peacock's hand. "Nice to meet you, sir. We'll be going on our way. I can promise you that Hobie here has learned his lesson."

"You'd better be right," Mr. Peacock said in a quiet tone that was more threatening than a shout would have been.

Without looking up I just knew that white figure was there, trying her desperate signal in that dark window. What could I do? I didn't even dare look up again, the way Mr. Peacock was staring at me.

The Gazebo

As the sheriff drove back down the driveway of the Peacock Place, he glanced over at the little house that was the copy of the big one and smiled. "Gazebo," he said. "They call a thing like that a gazebo. Being rich must be pretty easy to take."

Even if it means being a prisoner in your own house? I asked myself silently, still feeling a little shaky from seeing that face in the window.

I felt him glance over at me, but I didn't look back. Something in my face must have told him I wasn't much interested in anything he had to say.

And I wasn't. I had more than I needed to think about right inside my own head.

I guess I was already building up to another trip back to the Peacock Place as Sheriff Higher and I rode toward home. I wasn't thinking about it that way. I was just feeling irritated and restless because so many things seemed wrong. It would have been easy enough if there had been one big thing I could put my finger on. There wasn't — all I had was a collection of silly little details that were adding up until I couldn't handle them.

I had that sense of complete helplessness that comes with the very worst kind of nightmare. One of those dreams in which you see something horrible about to happen. You scream to warn people. You can feel that scream tear through your own throat, but all the time you know that you aren't making a sound. You are helpless to warn them, even while you keep on screaming.

Screaming at Sheriff Higher wasn't going to do any good. He'd already made up his mind. And at the rate I was going, Miss Peacock's silent appeals through that high window weren't going to help her, either. This was her nightmare, and mine, and the sheriff sitting beside me in his cruiser might have been made of stone for all the help he was going to be.

The radio chattered along, and the sheriff broke into its flow once in a while to give an order. Then, as he pulled in to the curb by our house, he glanced over at me.

"Just for the record, I didn't think much of your apology."

"I didn't break the window," I told him.

He shook his head, and his tone almost held an appeal. "How do you think that sounds, Hobie?

53

Mr. Peacock is the same as a stranger around here. Why would he make up a story like that? Why should he lie?"

"I don't know," I told him.

"It's his word against yours," he reminded me.

"I know it," I told him. Then recklessly, "And you only have that man's word that he's Miss Peacock's brother. He sure looks a lot younger than I thought he would. And meaner," I added.

He grinned at that, and nodded. "He's in good shape all right, but Miss Peacock did only have one brother and he was a lot younger than she was.

"Besides," he added after a minute, "Anderson must have seen him and recognized him, or he would never have gone off like he did to South Carolina."

After I got out and started for the front porch, the sheriff called after me. "If it makes you feel any better, I intend to keep an eye on things out there until Mr. Anderson brings Miss Peacock home. But you stay away away from that place, you hear me?"

It didn't make me feel any better, and I heard him.

It didn't really matter whether old Snake Arm was Miss Peacock's brother or not. Anybody who would treat a kid like that, glare at him, call him

54

names, and lie about him, sure couldn't be trusted with a frail, little old woman who he already thought was crazy.

The TV was blaring away all by itself in an empty room. I shut it off and went to look for Pat. I met her in the hall just outside the bathroom door. She was carrying a big armload of towels and bottles and jars. A ribbon was holding her hair back from her face, which was covered with something that looked like chocolate pudding.

"Mud mask," she explained at my startled look. "I'll be out in a half hour. I'm going to take a bath."

"With all that stuff?" I challenged her.

She peered down at the things she was carrying.

"What do you mean all that stuff?" She juggled the bottles around. "That's just bath oil and skin freshener and —"

"Never mind," I told her. "Listen, Pat," I dropped my voice. "I really need to talk to you."

"I'll be out in half an hour. Just half an hour." Her tone was airy. Then she added, "Promise."

While I waited, I fixed Shadow's food in the kitchen. Mrs. Kelley was humming to herself as she pulled open the oven door. She blinked, and blew a breath out as the wave of hot air hit her face.

"My, doesn't that smell good?" she asked. "Meat loaf and baked potatoes."

I smiled back, because I really like her, even if she can't cook. I like meat loaf as well as the next kid, which isn't very much. I love baked potatoes with their skins all crispy, and the inside crumbling under sour cream and chives. But Mrs. Kelley doesn't bake potatoes, she steams them. When they come out of that aluminum foil, they are mushy and wet, and taste like the dirt they grew in.

Never mind, I told myself. It was Saturday night and Mom would be home in just one more day. I would live.

"I'm sure looking forward to tonight," she chattered on, as I poured hot water on Shadow's kibbles. "My son and his wife from over by Decatur are stopping by to visit after the dance. I hope that won't bother you."

She could have entertained everybody in Illinois for all I cared. But it was spooky to me to have her chattering on like that, when my own head was full of something so dangerous and important. The contrast was too great between where I had been and where I was now.

The more normal everything seemed at my own house, the more strange and threatening my memory of the Peacock Place was. How could Pat be splashing around in there, getting ready for a dance, and Mrs. Kelley be humming about her happy evening ahead, while only a few miles away behind that killer-hedge Miss Peacock was trapped, with nobody even trying to do anything about it but me?

"Don't worry about me," I told Mrs. Kelley. "I'll probably be out at Ben's, anyway." Before she could reply, I let myself outside to give Shadow his dinner while it was still warm.

Shadow thinks it is impolite to eat when someone is watching. He kept wagging his tail and looking at me until I walked out to the back fence to let him eat in peace. When he was through, he bounded up, licking his chops, and I threw a stick for him until I thought the half hour was up.

What I failed to realize was that dinner would be ready at the same time that Pat would be through with her bath. She came to the table with a towel on her head, smelling of everything in all those bottles and jars at once. Her face had turned a nice pink from the mud mask, and her eyes shone the way they do when she is really happy.

She knew I wanted to talk to her, but she kept on chattering to Mrs. Kelley about the evening ahead.

"We're going to have a real live band," she announced. "A professional one, not from our school. And all the old graduates will be there," she went on. "And we get to lead the grand march."

Mrs. Kelley was right in there, telling what band had played at her first dance, and who she had gone with, and what she had worn. Halfway through dinner I couldn't stand it any longer. I excused myself, and went to the phone in Mom and Dad's room.

Maybe Pat could forget about Miss Peacock by rubbing stuff all over her face and getting dressed for a dance, but I couldn't. I rang Ben's number and hoped that he'd answer, instead of his mother who would be sure to ask me how I liked the parade. It was Ben all right.

"I have a question — " I said.

"Hey," he interrupted. "I looked all over and didn't see you today at the parade."

"I saw you," I told him. "You looked great, and so did Tony. I have a question."

"Yeah?" he asked, his voice sounding pleased and happy because of what I had said.

"Has your dad taken his horses to the Royal yet?" I asked.

"It's too early," he said. "He plans to leave about Thursday. Why did you ask?"

I had asked because I couldn't figure out why Caliph Haroun had been left, if the other Peacock horses had been taken away to the Royal like the sheriff said. I couldn't tell him that.

"I just wondered," I said lamely. "I thought somebody said the Peacock horses had already gone, but it sounded pretty early."

"It sure is too early," he said. "Somebody has

their dates mixed up. And why would they take the others without Caliph Haroun?"

"You got a point," I told him. "Thanks a lot."

I heard Mrs. Kelley calling me back to the table, but I sat there a minute anyway, just thinking.

Fishy, fishy, fishy. Miss Peacock was supposed to be off in South Carolina, and instead she was rocking like a clown in her upstairs window. The Peacock horses were supposed to be away at the Royal, but it didn't start for several more days. Mr. Peacock had left here as a young man thirty years ago, and still didn't have a gray hair in his head.

"Hobie." Mrs. Kelley's tone was moving toward cross. "You get on in here if you want chocolate pudding."

I groaned at the thought of chocolate pudding after the way Pat's face had looked before her bath. But chocolate pudding from a box is something that no one can spoil.

"What were you doing anyway?" Mrs. Kelley grumbled, as she set the sherbert dish in front of me.

"Talking to Ben," I told her.

She nodded, just presuming that she knew what we had been talking about. "You will be home early, won't you?"

I remembered how late she had waited up for Pat and me other times. "I thought I'd take some things, in case I wanted to spend the night," I told her.

Pat was off in some sort of fog, not hearing me, not hearing anything but her own thoughts, which had to be pretty sickening from the way she simpered at her pudding spoon.

Getting away to go back to the Peacock Place had been almost too easy. I rode my bike down the drive, and started out toward the country. I didn't really trust anything that came that easy. Besides, I didn't have any real plan for what I would do once I got out to the Peacock Place, except to watch what was going on. Pat's words had sunk deeper than she probably meant them to. If anything happened to Miss Peacock, it would be my fault if I didn't at least try to help her. But how?

The closer I got to the Peacock Place, the dumber my going out there seemed. Even if old Snake Arm decided to do something to Miss Peacock, what could I do about it? Run for help? Get in touch with the sheriff, and get another lecture on trespassing for my pains?

I got off my bike and walked it past the Peacock Place to the edge of the forest preserve. We don't have the greatest streetlights in the world in our town, but I sure missed them when I got out in that preserve and began stumbling over my own feet.

Even the sky was no help. The sliver of a moon that hung to the left and back of the house kept disappearing behind thin strands of black clouds. A couple of very bluish stars hung listlessly against that blackness.

I laid my bike flat in the dry stream bed, and walked back down to the road. Having gone into the Peacock Place with the sheriff, I knew that by crawling under the gate and staying close to the left I would be in the shadows of trees all the way to that little house the sheriff called a gazebo. That would be a perfect place to watch from, hidden in behind those posts and vines.

I had left home a little after seven. The dial of my watch glowed faintly under my cuff when I checked it the first time. It was a quarter after eight, and it seemed as if I had been there forever. I decided that peacocks go to bed with the chickens, because there wasn't a squeak out of them. There were bug noises and rustling in the leaves behind me that I told myself was a rabbit instead of a snake. Some night bird called from the hedge by the forest preserve and brought an answering cry.

The house was dark, except for a dim light in the second story. I decided it must be a hall light, because it didn't really light any one room.

When I heard the stable door open I crouched down hard, keeping my eyes on that widening triangle of light. Faint music drifted to where I was as the snake-arm man walked briskly to the house, leaving the door open. He returned, carrying something that looked like a pot of coffee. The music stopped when the door closed behind him.

There were three of us there, I decided: the woman in the house, that man who claimed to be Mr. Peacock, and myself. And there weren't any horses. If those horses weren't at the Royal, where would they be? And where were the men who took care of them?

It was just chilly enough so that I huddled down inside my jacket and curled up against a post. I was conscious of dozing off now and then, but I also knew that the slightest sound was going to bring me awake again.

I heard a little traffic go by on the road once in a while and a dog barking a long way off. The next time I yawned and checked my watch it was almost nine o'clock. The Homecoming Dance would last really late, and then Mrs. Kelley's family would be coming in. Pat had special permission to be out until twelve, so that she and her friends could go for sandwiches after the dance.

Then I heard the sound of a vehicle slowing

down, instead of passing right by. I felt my breath get short as it stopped at the bottom of the drive. The metal gate clanged as it was swung open. It was exactly nine by my watch.

I could tell it wasn't an ordinary car from the way it sounded in the drive, but I didn't recognize the Peacock horse van until the lights of a second car shone on the bright fan on its side. The moment the van reached the stable, the man who called himself Mr. Peacock came out and stood in the headlights of the van. The car that had followed waited back in the drive, its motor running.

The Stables

The minute the driver of the horse van stepped down into the gleam of the headlights I felt myself relax all over. I knew that man. That was Second Deputy Ames, who had ridden Caliph Haroun at the head of the Homecoming Parade. He lived on a farm not too far from where Ben did, and he was really liked by everyone in Ben's family. The sheriff had said that Ames had taken Caliph Haroun home to groom and ride in the Homecoming Parade. This was a crazy time of night to be bringing the horse back to his stable, but at least something was making sense for a change.

Something, probably the sound of the car in the drive, had started up the peacocks. They were yelling in that coarse, threatening way from the fenced yard they had run to from Shadow. This place sure didn't need a burglar alarm with those crazy birds carrying on like that at every little noise.

I couldn't hear what Deputy Ames and Mr. Peacock were saying, but it was obvious that they were exchanging greetings, and that Deputy Ames didn't see anything strange about this man who claimed to be Mr. Peacock.

They talked only a minute or two before Deputy Ames walked back, opened the back of the van, let down the ramp, and began to unload the horse. Caliph Haroun's white coat gleamed in the light as he backed down the ramp. Then he whinnied, and danced a little in place, as if he knew he was home and was glad to be there. Deputy Ames stroked him on the neck fondly, before he handed the reins to Mr. Peacock.

Then, wishing Mr. Peacock a good-night, Deputy Ames walked back and got into the car that was still waiting in the drive with its motor running.

As I said, I had really relaxed when I saw it was Deputy Ames there in the van with Caliph Haroun. It only took me a minute to realize that I had relaxed too fast. The car that had come to take Deputy Ames back home cruised slowly up to circle the drive and head back toward the road. As the car turned, its headlights swept the hedge, the lawn, and the gazebo where I was hiding.

That light was like a bath of terror. I never felt so exposed in my whole life. I felt as if every freckle on my face, and every torn place on my jeans, was visible for about a hundred miles. I felt like a bug on a pin, being held up to a lamp.

I didn't have many choices. I could figure that Mr. Peacock had seen me and make a run for the woods along the road where I could hide. Or I could freeze there like a rabbit on the chance that Mr. Peacock, back there at the stable door with Caliph Haroun, had not been looking my way.

I made the wrong decision.

Deputy Ames' car had barely passed me when I heard a muffled curse. Blinded by the glare from those headlights I couldn't see Mr. Peacock, but I heard the scrape of running feet along the cinder path and knew he was coming toward me.

I scrambled to my feet and started to run out of the gazebo. If I could get out of that place I would be in the darkness. Only a few yards of lawn lay between the gazebo and the staggered line of big trees that concealed the Peacock property from the road. I didn't have far to go to get a running chance.

I might even have gotten away if it hadn't been autumn. The floor of that gazebo was littered with dry leaves that had fallen from the vines, or been blown in there by the wind. Those leaves were crisp, and dry enough to make the painted wooden floor of the gazebo as slippery as glass. When I slid and went down, I went scooting across the floor and crashed against the railing. I don't know whether I twisted my right knee, or just struck it so hard against the wooden post that it almost cracked. Any other time I would have yelled at anything that hurt so much. Instead, I swallowed my pain and tried to struggle back onto my feet.

I didn't make it in time. Before I took a single step, Mr. Peacock was there.

I have seen some pretty angry grown-ups in my life. When Dad is about to blow, a little warning twitch appears at the side of his right eye, and Pat and I know it's time to lie low. Mom's mouth gets skinny and tight, and she calls you by your whole name — Patricia or Hobart. The difference between them and Mr. Peacock was that he was being angry like a little kid, not trying to hold it back at all or stay in control of himself.

His face flushed an ugly red under his suntan, and those weird eyes simply flashed with fury. He was across that wooden floor in three steps, and grabbed me up from where I had skidded into the railing. He jerked me to my feet and slapped me, all in one motion. It hurt like everything, a long line of hurt from the side of my head clear down through my shoulder. I don't even know whether I cried out. I don't think I had time to before he grabbed me by both shoulders, shook me hard, and threw me back against one of the posts that held up the roof of the gazebo. I hit the post with the back of my head so hard that I could hear it crack. Either the blow or the pain made me suddenly so dizzy that I couldn't stand up. I just slid down that post, and hit the floor hard with my ankle twisted under me.

Snake Arm hit me at least twice again, knocking my head first one way and then the other, when I heard another man's voice calling urgently.

"Cal," I heard. "Lay off that child. Let him alone."

Instead, the man with the snake tattoo leaned down and grabbed me by the shoulders. He jerked me roughly to my feet and spun me around. I was dizzy, and staggered. He pushed me hard in the middle of my back, thrusting me toward the stairs. If I hadn't caught onto the post, I would have fallen getting down them.

"Get out of sight," he was yelling at the other man. Then, with his balled fist, he threatened me. "Get going, kid, or you'll wish you had."

I wasn't in any shape to argue, so I limped along as fast as I could, trying to stay ahead of his blows. As I went, I saw the man in the doorway of the stable step back into the darkness. Apparently I wasn't the only person scared of this man's brutal fury.

But just that quick glimpse I had caught of the other man shivered through me like recognition. That was the way I had imagined Mr. Peacock would look. The man who had stepped back from the light had been tall, with a great mane of snow white hair. He had been slender in a frail, elderly way, with his shoulders a little stooped. Even his voice, saying those few words, had sounded right. The accent was not quite American, but more the way Englishmen talk in plays on TV.

The man with the tattoo shoved me against the wall of the stable and glared at me. He seemed to have forgotten the other man. His mouth made an ugly shape when he talked, and he held his arms half bent, as if he wanted to go on beating on me, even though he had me in a place where I couldn't get away.

"You had to stick your nose in, didn't you?" he shouted. "Not a very fast learner, are you?"

Then he slapped me again, for no reason at all, a hard slap across the side of the head that made my ears ring.

"Now get," he said, whirling me around and shoving me down the cinder path. "Get, and get fast."

Walking wasn't that easy on my hurt knee, but he prodded me so hard in the back with his fist that I really tried. Caliph Haroun, whom the man had tied hastily to a post when starting off after me, stamped restlessly, and looked down at me as we passed. Snake Arm walked me past the open door where the van belonged, and the door where I had seen the white-haired man.

When he stopped, he jerked open a door and

flipped a switch. The single, large bulb hanging from the middle of the ceiling blinded me for a moment. But even in the glare of that sudden blaze, I recognized the place as a tack room. This was not only a bigger tack room than the one at Ben's house, it was also a whole lot neater.

A long row of saddles rested on sawhorses along one wall. Harnesses of every size were hung on pegs in rows on the opposite wall. Along the back wall ran a workbench with shelves above it. Glass containers along the shelves were filled with all kinds of things, metal mostly; what looked like buckles and fasteners and horseshoe nails. A bunch of wooden-handled tools littered the working surface, which was stained and cut from the tools.

After he shoved me into the room, the man with the tattoo glanced angrily around the place. Then, from a bin by the door, he pulled out a length of leather strapping about a half-inch wide. Spinning me around, he jerked my wrists together behind my back and bound them tight with the leather straps. Then, without warning, he shoved me so that I fell back on the floor. Kneeling swiftly, he bound my ankles and said, "There," in a satisfied tone. "That should keep you out of my hair long enough."

After backing to the door, he turned and studied the room carefully for a long minute, seeming to take in every detail with those intense blue eyes.

70

Then, unexpectedly, he stepped back into the room, pulled a riding crop from beside the door and struck the ceiling light bulb a sharp blow with the handle of the crop.

I gasped at the pop of the bulb. A shower of fine shattered glass fell all around me. I felt it gritting on the backs of my bound hands like angel's hair on Christmas trees. I stared at where the light had been. The thread inside the bulb did the weirdest thing. It glowed in a delicate twisted shape for a brief moment, then darkened so quickly that I wondered if I had imagined it. Crazy spinning orbs of light that were fuzzy around the edges spun in the darkness where the bulb had been. Then the room was absolutely dark, so dark that his voice seemed changed, even softened by it.

"Just in case," he laughed.

Then he pulled the door shut behind him, so that the darkness in the room was complete. I didn't move for a few minutes after he left. I was scared, and I hurt all over. When I was finally sure that he was gone for good, I twisted around there on the floor and looked toward the door.

The only window in the room was beside the door that opened onto the cinder path. It was very high and small, a narrow rectangular window designed more to air the dense leather smell from the room than to give light.

But at least I could see out of it. From there

on the floor the angle was right. I looked up and saw the outside of that big yellow house. And I could see two of the windows of the house, those high windows that had gotten me into this mess in the first place.

After a while, the peacocks settled down. The only sound I heard was a rumble of voices from the next room. I tried wriggling my hands to free them, but it hurt too much. That man might have only broken that light to keep me from turning it on for a signal, but he had done me more damage than he knew. When I felt something wet and sticky on my hands, I figured it had to be blood from the broken glass that had fallen and stuck in those leather bindings. The thought made me a little bit sick.

I didn't even try to get up, too much had happened too fast. It didn't seem possible that anyone would beat up a kid, shove him around and tie him up, then just go off and leave him forever and ever. I kept expecting to see the door open, or to have him yell at me, or make some violent noise out there. Instead, there was only that low rumble of voices, as calm as the way Mom and Dad's voices sounded when they talked on the porch on summer nights when they thought Pat and I were asleep.

After a long time with nothing happening, I tried to twist my head around to see my watch. It had to be midnight by now with all that had happened. I really hurt all over. If I had been a little kid I think I would have bawled. Instead, I tried to think of all the things people did that hurt this bad, things they did on purpose, and wouldn't cry about for the world. Football, that had to be one, or riding a bucking bronco.

Ben had been thrown from a horse once, when he tried to take his father's jumper over a fence out at the farm. He had walked like he was about a hundred years old for two whole weeks.

I looked up again at the dark window of that immense yellow house that loomed across the path. I felt my muscles stiffen, and forgot how they had been hurting the minute before. That window wasn't dark anymore. Instead, something vague and white was pressed against it. A face with hands on either side. She was there. Miss Peacock must have seen it all, and knew where I was. I had to get a signal to her. I had to get a signal to somebody to save both of us from whatever the snake-armed man had planned.

"Long enough," Cal had said. "This should hold you long enough."

I decided I had never heard a scarier phrase in my whole life.

The Cry of Peacocks

The tack room had a concrete floor. The longer I lay there, the colder and stiffer I got. I could feel the cold moving up through my body like mercury through a thermometer. My head started acting funny. If a thermometer measured how hot you were, what would you call something that measured how cold you got? And how cold would I have to get to be unable to walk again if I got free?

And what had the man with the tattoo meant by "enough time"?

Whatever he had meant, I couldn't just lie there and wait for it to happen.

I really went to work on getting my wrists free of those leather straps I was bound with. It wasn't easy, and it certainly wasn't comfortable. I just gritted my teeth and kept at it. I was sure that the dampness that I felt was my own blood. I knew from the pain that any skin left under those straps was strictly an accident. Only after what seemed like hours did it finally dawn on me that I was working on the wrong set of straps. Nothing in the world was going to make my hands skinny enough to work out of those loops. Maybe that wasn't true about my feet.

Dad calls my feet "a standing joke." He says he has seen clowns dressed in full costume who wore smaller shoes than I do. He says that if boys are like puppies, and grow up to the size of their feet, that he is going to change my name to St. Bernard and train me for rescue duty in the Swiss Alps.

I just laugh a lot and don't let it bother me. I know my feet are half again as long as Ben's, because we measured them. But Ben's feet are fat where mine are skinny, which gave me the great idea for getting loose.

My feet are so long and skinny that we can never really get tennis shoes narrow enough. If I could just snake one of those shoes off, maybe I could stand up and get off that cold floor.

The trouble with that idea was that I am really a good shoe-tier. I have enough trouble falling over my feet without fighting loose laces, too.

All the time I sat there scrubbing my feet together to try to work one of them loose, I kept wishing for more light in that tack room. Old Snake Arm really knew what he was doing when he broke that light bulb. I could have rolled over to the door, and maybe staggered onto my feet long enough to snap that light back on with my chin if he hadn't ruined the bulb.

But after a while you really do begin to see better in the dark. I decided that I was getting a delayed reaction to the bushels of carrot sticks Mom has served me in my life. When my eyes got better in the dimness, I studied every possible place in the room that anyone would put a flashlight. Ben's dad keeps a flashlight in their tack room. Dad keeps a flashlight in his workroom. It's worth your life to borrow it and not return it, because it's for emergencies.

Apparently Mr. Anderson didn't believe in emergencies. If there was a flashlight in that room, it was hidden away inside something. But Mr. Anderson did believe in mice. I figured that out from studying the row of glass jars on the shelf above the workbench. In among the jars of metal things was a peanut butter jar full of those old-fashioned wooden stick matches that you use to start campfires. I first saw matches in a jar like that out at Ben's house. They were on his mom's kitchen shelf, right next to a peanut butter jar with peanut butter still in it.

"Who eats matches?" I asked him.

"Nobody, silly," he said. "They are for when the electricity goes out in storms, and stuff."

"But why didn't you leave them in the box?"

"Mice chew on them and start fires," he said.

"Rodent arsonists?" I asked, breaking up at the idea.

He gave me a disgusted look, and took the jar and put it down under the sink with the cleaning supplies. "When you live on a farm with all this hay and dried wood, fire isn't all that funny," he told me. "Farmers stay on the lookout for fires, just like forest rangers do."

I didn't try to make any more jokes about it because he took it so seriously, but I always think of rodent arson when I see matches in a jar.

My campaign to get a foot loose finally succeeded. I got one of the laces undone by rubbing the top of one shoe against the other one. Then I pinned down the end of that shoelace and tugged my foot away until the knot gave. I would have given out a yell if I hadn't been conscious of those two men still talking quietly in the next room.

The heel of that foot was really bruised and sore when it finally came free, but the second foot came out without any problem.

I stood up and bounced in my stocking feet for a minute, before I remembered those fragments of broken light bulb that were all over the floor. I wouldn't have felt them even if they had cut through my socks, because my feet already had pins and needles from being tied up so long. But I felt great anyway. For one thing I was up off that icy floor. For another, maybe I really did have a chance of getting out of there in one piece.

Naturally, the first thing I did was go over to the window. By standing on tiptoe I could see out. Mostly I could just see straight — the side of the house and the bushes around it. But at least there was light coming from both sides from those dim lantern-shaped lights that were spaced over the doors of the stables.

The first thing I looked for was Miss Peacock. Sure enough, that pale face was in the same window where I had seen it before. Only this time Miss Peacock wasn't just looking. She was shaking her head back and forth in a really desperate way, as if to warn me.

The only thing she could be warning me about was being seen. I dropped down fast to hide myself. The sight of her had made my heart start thumping in that loud, scary way again. But over the hammering in my own chest I heard the scrunch of feet along the cinder path outside my window. I held my breath.

When the footsteps stopped right outside, I felt my heart plunge. What if Cal was looking in to see that I was still tied up? What if he realized I was free and came back in and bound me up tighter? I was suddenly grateful for the same darkness that I had been so cross about earlier. I figured that he couldn't see anything at all, and just gave up trying to see into that darkness, because the steps turned back and faded away. I can't believe that he didn't hear my heartbeat clear through that wooden door.

Squatted down on the floor the way I was, I saw something I hadn't noticed before. Just inside the door, next to the floor, was a low metal V fastened securely to the wall. It looked like a boot scraper that you clean your shoes on before you go from the stable into the house. Ben has one shaped just the same on his back steps, except that his is made out of wood. All you could get off the one at Ben's house was splinters, but it was worth a try to see if those blades were sharp enough to cut leather.

Boy, did I hate to get back down on that cold floor. But I did let myself down, and squirmed around with my back to the boot scraper until I could feel the metal against my hands. I didn't know what to do, except just sit there sawing away, hoping that I would loosen a place until it was weak enough to give.

I had forgotten about the peacocks until a big clatter started outside again. It took me a minute to get up on my feet, and a minute more to get over so I could see out of the window. The men in the next room fell silent as if they, too, had been startled by the racket from the poultry yard.

Then above the clatter of those birds, I heard the unmistakable purr of a car motor coming slowly up the drive, and the rough crunch of wheels turning on gravel. At first I thought the light outside was just the headlamps of an ordinary car. Then I realized that what I saw was a beam, a wide, white beam of light that was moving around the property, flashing into the bushes by the house, and passing over the window of the tack room, flooding the room with light for one brief minute.

Sheriff Higher.

What had lit the tack room like day was the movable floodlight on Sheriff Higher's police car. I tried jumping up and down in hope that he would notice something moving behind my window. It was no use. The light had passed my window and was gone. Already it was flashing back along the stables toward where the peacocks were yelling alarm. Then, as swiftly as it had come, it was gone. I could tell from the sound of the motor receding that the cruiser had drifted around the curve of the circular drive, and was moving back down the drive toward the road.

I turned, really sick at heart. Sheriff Higher had told me that he would keep an eye on the place, but I hadn't really thought he would. Now that he had seen everything looking okay, he would probably go home and go to bed.

Unless he was really looking for me. Boy, was it exciting to think that maybe he was actually out looking for me.

Maybe Ben had called, and asked to speak to me. Mrs. Kelley would know that I wasn't at his house. Given all the horrors she imagines, she would call the sheriff right off and report me missing. Naturally, he would come straight out here looking.

I really had my hopes built up for a minute there. Then I realized that even if he knew I was missing, he would figure he had looked out here and start searching somewhere else.

I turned away from the window really discouraged. I had already been trapped in there for the better part of the night, and I wasn't any closer to getting out than I had been when Cal first tied me up.

Then I saw that funny little glow of light at my feet — my watch. I had cut my watchband loose with that boot scraper, and it was lying there staring up at me from the floor. I squatted down and looked at it in disbelief.

I would have sworn I had been locked up in that tack room for hours. My watch hands pointed to exactly ten o'clock. Deputy Ames had brought Caliph Haroun back to the stable at nine o'clock. They had taken their time talking and unloading that horse, so it must have been about nine-fifteen before Deputy Ames finally got into his car and left. I had only been in the tack room for forty-five minutes.

That was when I really gave up. I decided I didn't have the stubborn courage that Miss Peacock had. I was tired and sleepy, and I hurt all over. My hands felt crusty from being all cut up with that glass. And I was thirsty, too, now that I thought about it. I decided I was just going to give up and lie there until something happened.

That wouldn't even work. Did you ever try to go to sleep with both hands tied behind your back? There isn't a single good way to lie. You can't lie on your back, because you crunch your tied-up hands. And if you turn over on your stomach, your arms ache. When you curl on your side, you feel like you're going to roll all the time.

The only sensible thing to do was to keep at it with the boot scraper. I told myself I was only getting my hands untied so I could sleep as I backed over to that silly metal V and started sawing away at the leather again.

Voices Beyond the Wall

In order to get the bindings on my wrists hooked over the sharp blade of the boot scraper, I had to crouch down with my head jammed up against the wall. Earlier in the evening I had heard the steady rumble of quiet voices from that adjoining room. But there hadn't been a sound, not even a whisper, from in there while the sheriff's car cruised around the driveway throwing his light everywhere.

By the time I gave up trying to sleep and got myself down by that foot scraper again, there was plenty to hear behind the wall. The men were not only talking again, they were moving things around in that careless, fast way you do when you are in a hurry. The floor beneath me vibrated from heavy, rapid footsteps. Then I heard the door opened, and slammed shut again.

I stretched myself up to the window to try to see what was going on out there. I couldn't see much from that silly high window, but after a few minutes I heard the growl of a motor being started up. Then Cal backed the horse van far enough out into the driveway so that I could see it from my window. He stopped the van in the driveway and got out.

The slender, white-haired man that I thought of as the real Mr. Peacock stood watching while Cal let down the ramp and went back to the stable. Under that dim light the old man looked very pale and tired. He stood motionless with a kind of sad look on his face as his companion returned, leading Caliph Haroun.

The big white horse obviously had his own ideas about being dragged out of his stall in the middle of the night. He fought the lead, balking and jerking his head this way and that, as he was tugged along. When he whinnied loudly, and bared his teeth at this rough handling, Cal cursed furiously at him.

I've seen Ben and his dad try to load balky horses into their horse trailer. Since none of their horses has anything like Caliph's spirit, I figured that Cal was in for a fight before he got Caliph in that van. I had no idea how much fight that big champion had in him.

Caliph Haroun balked completely at the bottom of the ramp. He fought the halter so furiously that I wondered how he could stand that bit being bounced around in his mouth like that. Cal acted as if he didn't care if he tore that horse's head off, as long as he got him loaded.

They reached a standoff. Cal was using all his strength, and the horse wasn't giving an inch. I don't know what Cal had in his mind, but apparently he loosened the halter for a minute. Clearly, he wasn't the only one who was thinking. Caliph Haroun looked as if he had just been waiting for that instant of relief from the pressure. In a flash, the horse reared up, pawing the air and slashing with his front hooves at the man holding his halter.

Cal let go and scrambled away, half crawling and half running from the horse's attack. When Caliph continued to come after him, Cal ran for the cab of the van. He barely got there in time to slam the door between himself and the furious horse.

Caliph Haroun's anger passed as swiftly as it had come. Trailing his halter, he ran a couple of swift graceful circles around the deep lawn before stopping down by the gazebo. He dropped his graceful head, and began to crop the grass contentedly, only stopping once in a while to stare at the van.

Only after the horse had been calm a long time did Cal slide carefully out of the cab. His face was twisted with fear and anger as he began to yell at the older man.

"Get a whip, Peacock!" he shouted. "Get a whip,

and give me a hand with that murderous beast!"

"You can't mark that horse with a whip," the old man told him. "Let up. Give him a few more minutes to settle down."

"You and your minutes," the younger man scoffed. "You think we got all night? Thanks to that nosy kid, that hick sheriff of yours could come prowling back here any minute. This rotten beast has got to be on the road and gone."

The old man, who had simply stepped back a few feet when the horse reared, held his place and ignored this tirade. Then he began to move slowly across the lawn toward the horse. "Here, fellow," he called, looking directly at Caliph Haroun. The horse, his ears pricked forward and his eyes careful, danced away a little, before standing to watch Mr. Peacock approach.

"That's a fellow," the white-haired man continued to murmur as he drew nearer. A few feet away he paused, knelt, and plucked a handful of grass from the edge of a flower bed. At first he didn't offer the horse the grass. Instead, he simply stood holding it, and looking the animal in his eyes.

Caliph Haroun switched his head from side to side as if he were saying no. Mr. Peacock continued to stand very still, as if he didn't understand what the horse meant. Then, almost as if drawn by the calmness in the old man's face, Caliph Haroun took one step and then a second, toward Mr.

Peacock, until he was standing close enough to be patted if the older man had wanted to stretch out his hand.

"Grab the halter!" Cal yelled from the van. "Don't be a fool. Get hold of him!"

The horse turned to stare at the sound, but Mr. Peacock didn't look around or act as if he had heard a thing.

In no time at all, Caliph Haroun was delicately pulling the strands of grass from the old man's hand with his lips.

"The halter!" Cal kept yelling furiously from a safe spot by the van.

Instead of reaching for the dangling reins, the old man stroked the horse along his neck, the way Deputy Ames had, and he patted the smooth flesh by his mane.

"Good fellow," he kept saying. "Good Caliph, that's a fellow." When Mr. Peacock finally took up the reins and began to lead the horse back across the lawn, Caliph Haroun, still chewing contentedly, followed like a trained dog.

Mr. Peacock was still talking to the horse as he led him up the ramp and into the van. Cal, his face flushed with anger, watched silently from a safe distance.

"What anybody wants with a killer horse like that beats me," he said, as Mr. Peacock came back out of the van, and closed the door behind Caliph

Haroun. "Or any of those nags," he added after a minute. "But who am I to argue with that much money?"

I realized that I hadn't seen Cal smile before. It was just as well. I've seen frowns that looked friendlier than his smile.

"In any case we can finish up here now," the old man said. "What shall we do about the boy?"

His companion laughed. "Let him rot. And that crazy sister of yours, too. Somebody will either find all of you in time or they won't. Anderson's due back in a week, isn't he? The three of you can hold your breath until then, for all I care."

I saw the gun before old Mr. Peacock did. Cal slid it out of his jacket pocket so smoothly that it was there in his hand, short and blunt and ugly, before I realized what he was doing. Old Mr. Peacock stared at it and then at him, as if he was trying to make some sense of what was going on.

Cal held the gun carelessly and laughed. "You planned too good, old fellow. Sending Anderson away was the smartest thing. He would have smelled a rat when we shipped the rest of the horses out early with a strange crew. But with the buyers waiting, and the papers here in my pocket for them and this killer, I don't need you. Nobody needs you that I can see. As your agent I can deliver the horses and collect the money. Now move."

Even as Mr. Peacock tried to speak, Cal prodded him roughly toward the cinder path with the gun in his back. "Move it, I said. I haven't got all night."

"Listen, Cal — " Mr. Peacock protested, his face stark white under the dim stable light.

"You listen," the man broke in. "It ain't like you didn't lead me on. Look at the stuff you got me into. That sheriff stood right there and looked me in the eye for half an hour. He'll know my mug shot anywhere. And that sister of yours. I've fixed her now so she won't get in my way. You told me she was out of her mind, and I discover that she's no crazier than you proved yourself to be when you trusted me. That old biddy came within an ace of giving us away by signaling with her cane to that carrot-headed kid. If I hadn't jerked her out of that window — "

He broke off, glanced at the van, and cursed. "Enough jabber. You can always pray somebody comes looking for that worthless kid. I only need twelve hours to collect the money and get away clean. You'll never make it out of that stable fast enough to stop me."

With that he jabbed the gun fiercely into the old man's back, and they disappeared from my view.

When I glanced up, I realized that I had not been the only witness to this scene. The white face, scarcely more than a blur behind the dark glass, had been watching with me, and had seen all that I had seen. I wanted to cry for her as well as myself.

I didn't really think anything worse could happen. I was wrong. As I turned from the window, I heard a pained cry from the next room.

"That should keep you quiet for a while, you old fool," Cal said in a tone of satisfaction.

Then I heard Mr. Peacock fall heavily to the floor. It was amazing that so frail a man could hit the floor that hard. That time Cal didn't slam the door. Instead it shut quietly and I heard the rattle of the key in the lock.

After a long moment, the motor of the horse van kicked to life, tires crunched on the gravel of the drive, and then the sounds faded away.

A Blaze of Light

Cal was gone then, and he had taken Caliph Haroun along with him. And the other horses were gone, not to the American Royal the way Sheriff Higher had said, but to some buyer who would give the money to Cal as Mr. Peacock's agent.

That thought really hurt. From what I had seen of old Mr. Peacock, he didn't seem a man who would lock his sister in as a prisoner, and steal and sell her possessions. But I had heard it with my own ears, along with all that other stuff I wish I had never heard.

So now there were three of us: Miss Peacock locked into that room upstairs, old Mr. Peacock unconscious beyond the wall, and me with my wrists still tied together. I wished I could forget Cal's voice out there in the drive as he held that gun on Mr. Peacock.

"Let him rot. And that crazy sister of yours.

Somebody will find all of you in time, or they won't."

They'd find me, I told myself. When I didn't come home in the morning from Ben's house, Pat and Mrs. Kelley would start looking for me. But who would think to look for me here? Once the sheriff might have, but after making rounds like that and seeing nothing, he wouldn't be apt to try the same place again.

Rounds. I looked at my watch. It was twenty minutes until eleven. Cal had been in a hurry because he was afraid of the sheriff coming around again. Was it possible Sheriff Higher was really going to make rounds like the policeman did of the locked stores downtown? If so, the sheriff would come cruising through here again at eleven o'clock.

If Sheriff Higher came back, one of us had to be ready to signal him, either me, or Mr. Peacock next door.

That was when I made my really big mistake. Instead of spending every one of those precious minutes working at getting my hands free, I went over and kicked the wall between the tack room, and the room where Mr. Peacock had been knocked out.

After kicking the wall as hard as I could and then listening, I began shouting at the man in the next room. Nothing. The silence from the other side of the wall made me a little sick.

I remembered how heavy it had sounded when Mr. Peacock fell. What if Cal had only meant to knock Mr. Peacock out and had really killed him? What if he had hurt him so bad that Mr. Peacock would go and die if he didn't get to a doctor?

Boy, I was getting as wild an imagination as Pat had! And all that time what I should have been doing was getting my wrists cut free so that I could get the sheriff's attention if he did come back the way Cal thought he would.

I was down there on the floor desperately sawing that strap back and forth on the boot scraper when I heard the peacocks begin that wild clamoring of theirs and saw a flash of light on the window.

I tried to jump up and get my hands loose from the V of metal, but instead, I lost my balance and fell really hard across the floor. For a minute there it felt as if my hands were being torn off. Then, as I braced myself to get up, I let out a yell. My hands hurt so much that I hadn't even realized I had gotten them free. That good, solid tug I had given the strap when I fell had finally broken it. The light flashed again, brighter this time.

I jumped to my feet and ran to the window. I know I never moved that fast before in my life. I grabbed something wooden off the wall and hit the window glass with it hard. That explosive noise of glass breaking made my ears hurt for a minute, the same sound that had started this whole business. Broken glass clunked down all around me as I stuck my fist out through that window, and waved frantically. But from the window I saw the taillights of the sheriff's car as it drifted away down the drive toward the road, flashing its searchlight in the bushes and around the gazebo.

That brilliant light had flashed against the window, just as it had done an hour earlier. When I saw the sheriff's car disappear around the trees to go out onto the road, I grabbed my watch from the floor and looked at it. Sheriff Higher had come back on the stroke of eleven o'clock.

Eleven o'clock on the dot. Twice now he had come exactly on the hour. That had to mean he would come one more time. Maybe after midnight he would quit, but he had to come one more time. He had to.

What I had to do was make a foolproof signal that he couldn't miss, no matter what. I had one hour to figure out a signal he couldn't possibly miss.

Now that I had my hands free, I could have stacked stuff up and crawled out that window, if it had been any more than a silly little slit.

A flag to wave was a possibility, but it had to be something that would show up against the yellow of the painted stable. The only cloths in the

94

place were some white cotton rags and some of those chamois leathers that Dad and I use to polish the car after we wash it. My sweat shirt was even a pale putty color. I wouldn't have any problem getting something to tie the flag to. I could take my pick of the riding crops in the barrel in the corner. I was still staring all around that room, looking for something bright or dark that I could use to make a flag, when I saw that peanut butter jar full of matches.

Fire! The very thought scared me.

Starting a fire is an even worse thing for a kid to do than breaking a window. But when the sheriff came back it would be midnight. Pat would be coming home from the dance all fuzzy-headed, like she had been at dinner. She and Mrs. Kelley would sit and talk about really important things, like who danced with whom and what they had on. Then they would go off to bed and that would be it until morning.

I decided to test the matches. If they worked, then I would use them as a last resort. Once I knew that they worked, I might be able to think of something smarter before the hour got away from me.

Everybody makes casual remarks about Einstein's theory of relativity. All I know about it is that Pat says it explains that time changes under different conditions. I will certainly never doubt that again. Earlier in the evening, with the floor feeding its arctic chill through me, and both my arms and legs tied up, forty-five minutes had seemed like two or three hours. Now, with only an hour to make a surefire, foolproof signal that Sheriff Higher couldn't miss in a hundred years, the minutes practically knocked me down zooming by.

I got the jar of matches down and tried one out. It was old and rotten, and the head dropped off to blaze into nothing in a bright, blue flame on the floor. A sharp smell, sort of like rotten eggs, filled the room. The next one I tried worked fine. I set the jar over by the window, tied two of the cotton rags to a riding crop, and walked around that room looking at everything with the idea of using it as a signal. Nothing, absolutely nothing in that room could be stuck out that window, or thrown out into the driveway to catch the sheriff's eye.

Once I thought I heard a groan from the next room, but when I went to listen, I couldn't hear anything. I rapped really hard on the wall, but Mr. Peacock didn't answer.

Miss Peacock was gone from her window upstairs, too. Now there was only me and those scary minutes that stretched until midnight.

If there had been a lamp in there, or even a candle, I could have had some light. I might have found something there to read, even if it was only something about horses.

More than anything I didn't want to think about those two old people locked up and nobody knowing to look for them.

Maybe old Mr. Peacock deserved some of what he was getting. It was plain enough that Mr. Peacock himself had been at the bottom of this big plot. "You planned too well," Cal had said. It was Mr. Peacock who had sent Mr. Anderson off on that long vacation, told Cal that Miss Peacock was crazy, and found somebody who would pay a lot of money for Caliph Haroun and the other Peacock horses. Even if he was Miss Peacock's brother, that was still stealing. But to be lying in there hurt, and maybe dead was more than he deserved.

As for the woman upstairs . . . I groaned, and got up and walked around. I only had to get through about twenty-three minutes more, and everything would be straightened out. The sheriff would come, see my burning flag, let me out, and send the police after that van before Cal could "get beyond reach." But poor Miss Peacock had lost her horses; she would find out awful things about her brother, and would probably be scared of her shadow for the rest of her life.

Every once in a while I banged on the wall, and waited for the answer that never came.

Finally, in spite of everything, I dozed off. I had sat in one of the saddles, thinking that would keep me awake. It didn't. I woke up with sort of a jump. I was icy cold, and had a sore place in my neck where my head had rolled over funny. When I looked down at my watch, I practically flew off that saddle. It was three minutes until midnight.

The first match wouldn't start. The second one burned the rag a little along the threads at the edge, but it wouldn't really catch. I was so scared that my plan wasn't going to work that my hand actually trembled with that last match.

It did the same thing, blackening the threads along the edge, but then a fine pale flame rose, and the fire began to move along the cloth toward the whip it was tied to. I held it out the window and waited.

Outside in the air that rag began to burn like a torch. Just as they had done when the sheriff's lights had whirled about the drive, those peacocks set up that terrible screaming clamor out in back.

The light blazed up from the cloth. I was half-way scared that it might put the overhang of the roof on fire. But I didn't dare pull it back in. It was one minute until midnight, and any second now Sheriff Higher would turn in from the road down there, and see my signal.

The Hands of the Clock

L it only by the dim light of the row of lamps
that were set along the length of the Peacock
stables, the view from my window had looked normal and proper, almost sleepy. The moment the
torch began to blaze, all that was changed. The
greedy, leaping flames took over the entire scene
in a matter of seconds. Things that had been
graceful and sensible one moment, turned fear-
some and misshapen right before my eyes.

The posts along the cinder path cast long, dark
shadows that angled out like heavy strands of some
giant spiderweb. The way the fire danced, instead
of blazing steadily, made the bushes and trees
seem to jerk and move, as if everything in the
whole yard had been magically brought to life.

You would have thought that at least I could
see more clearly. Even that was not true. The
gleaming yellow paint of the house acted almost
like a mirror, catching the fire and reflecting it
back to blind me. I couldn't tell whether Miss

Peacock was still watching because the glass of her window had become a blazing square of dancing points of light.

It was like being in the middle of the most horrifying TV movie in the world, and not being able to switch it off and go away.

The sheriff would be there. He had to be.

I watched the seconds crawl by on the hand of my watch, thirty seconds, forty-five, then all of the hands of my watch stood together for what seemed like the longest second in the history of the world. It was midnight.

As if to make up for that extra long pause, the second hand of the watch jerked on, and began a quickened path around the dial. I strained to try to see the angle of the drive where the sheriff's car lights should be showing. I told myself that the peacocks had even begun to scream louder, and that meant the sheriff's car was coming.

Kidding myself didn't help. Nothing was going to help. It got to be seven minutes after twelve, then ten, and then thirteen. I had been wrong about the sheriff making his rounds. I had been wrong to think that anyone would miss me. I had simply been wrong, wrong, wrong, from the first.

Then, just as I gave up on the sheriff ever coming in time to see my signal, the cloth burned itself out. Those flames that had changed the house and grounds to a scene of horror disappeared as swiftly as they had risen. The wad on the end of the stick was a black, wet-looking mass sparked with prickles of bright red spots like the eyes of animals at night.

The burned-out, blackened cloth went limp and soft, like a balloon emptied of air. It fell off the end of the whip to the ground, where I couldn't see it from that slit of a window.

I slid to the floor just like that burned up old rag had fallen to the ground. I had failed. I had tried everything I could think of, and some things I shouldn't have thought of, and still I had failed. The old man in the next room could be dying, or dead. Miss Peacock was hopelessly imprisoned, the same way he and I were.

It didn't really matter why the sheriff hadn't come. What mattered was that he wasn't there. And all that time, that rotten Cal was racing along the road somewhere with Caliph Haroun in the back of the Peacock van, on his way to maybe getting away with murder.

The only good thing I could think of was that things couldn't possibly be worse.

In fact, the smoke that still lingered in the room began to smell really good to me. It smelled like the fires Dad used to set in the fall, after we raked all the leaves off the yard into one big pile. Ben always came in and helped, because of the party afterward. Mom would bring a tray of buns and hot dogs and mustard out to the picnic table. After the leaves were all in a pile, Dad would light them, and we would cook the hot dogs on sticks until we were too full for anything but the marshmallows we roasted afterward.

Homesick is not just an expression, it's a real thing. That sweet autumn smell like burning leaves made me sick to be back home, and out of this cramped, dark room with the peacocks still shouting their heads off, even though my torch had died out.

I don't know how long it took for that growing light to get my attention. But it finally dawned on me that the back of the tack room was bathed with a steadily stronger light. I could read the labels on the lines of jars along the shelf, and pick out the tools as plain as day.

I leaped up and shot to the window. That would be Sheriff Higher; he had come after all. My torch was gone, and I still didn't have a flag, but I could scream maybe, or throw things out the window. I had to get his attention.

The minute I reached the window I knew that light was not coming from any spotlight on a police car. Now the spiderweb beyond my door was made of fire. There must have been more of those winking scarlet sparks in that burned-up rag than I thought. There had been enough to set fire to the dry grass where it fell.

That was what I had smelled, not burning leaves at all, but grass. Now, quick little tongues of flame shot out in all directions. They licked at the clumps of grass at the base of the poles along the walk. Fed by the dead vegetation, they ran in under the bushes along the side of the house, lit them from underneath, then swallowed whole bushes in fire. White smoke was billowing everywhere, the purest, whitest smoke I had ever seen, looping in great masses almost like clouds, hiding the house from me.

Hiding everything from me. It poured in through the broken window, and I began to cough hard from it. Everybody knows how dangerous breathing smoke like that is. I groped my way to the barrel where I had found the cloth to burn. I finally found one big enough to tie around my head and cover my mouth. By that time my eyes were all sore from it, and crying tears that I could feel soaking into the rag on my face.

I dropped to the floor because that was what the fire chief had taught us to do. Even as I did, I realized that I didn't care that much about saving myself then. Who was going to save that old man and Miss Peacock when those bushes around the house got hot enough to set the painted house on fire?

I never realized before how loud fire was, how it crackles and sizzles until you can't even think straight. Some of the noises I recognized: the brisk snap of burning timbers breaking; the hiss of burning paint; and always over everything, the screams of those peacocks. When the pounding noise began I thought it was just something else tumbling into the ashes. Then there was a screaming almost like the sound of a human voice.

Then I heard a noise that nobody could ever fool me on. Shadow. Shadow was barking his danger call. Shadow was out there in that fire looking for me.

I dragged myself through the smoke to the window and pulled myself up. I began to yell for all I was worth.

"There he is." The voice was Pat's. "Quick, Ben," I heard her say. "There he is."

Shadow. Pat. Ben. None of this made any sense. I felt those crazy tears burning their way out of my eyes as I shouted out to them.

"The door," I kept yelling, like a real simpleton. Someone was already pounding on the door. The sound of cracking wood came like a shot through the smoke in the room. Then Ben fell over the threshold into the room, splat on his face. A hammer or hatchet, or something heavy like that, flew out of his hand and spun across the floor to crash against the workbench on the far wall.

Plumes of Smoke

The minute I tore the cloth from my mouth to yell for help, the smoke got me. I was coughing helplessly as Ben rolled to his feet and started toward me. "Come on," he urged, grabbing for my arm. "Let's get out of here."

He couldn't know how great that open door looked to me after the hours just past. I tried to catch myself at the threshold, but missed the step in all that smoke. I tripped and went down on my face on the cinder path, with Ben right behind me.

Before I even saw anyone else out there, I smelled dog breath really close. Rough, hot tongues were licking me everywhere, my face, my hands. For one confused minute I thought I was imagining two Shadows telling me how glad they were that I was safe, and out of that tack room.

Only as I pulled myself up did I realize that the second tongue belonged to Ben's dog Stormy, who seemed just as excited as Shadow was to see me again.

How Ben and Pat had gotten there didn't even matter right then. I didn't even take time to thank them for saving my life. Instead, I jumped to my feet and raced for the door of the room where old Mr. Peacock was imprisoned.

"In here," I shouted to Ben. "Mr. Peacock is in here, and he might even be dead." Then remembering, I whirled around. "And the house," I told them desperately. "Miss Peacock is trapped up there in that house."

Ben, his face smudged with smoke, stared at me with his mouth half open. I guess none of it really made any sense to him right then. He frowned and looked at Pat.

She was crying. That black stuff she had put on around her eyes had gotten mixed with her tears and was running in jagged black streaks down her cheeks. She was dressed like a clown, with her party dress on under a down jacket, and old jeans pulled up underneath.

"Mr. Peacock?" Ben repeated, almost as if he didn't believe me. Then, glancing at the house, he said, "Miss Peacock? Up there?"

"We've got to get help," Pat said firmly. "Somebody's got to get to a phone."

Ben nodded, still looking awfully confused. Then he turned, and with his arm across his mouth, went back into the tack room. I would have yelled at him, but I didn't have time. In a second, he was back with the hammer he had used to break down the tack room door.

Instantly, he was there beside me. I was trying to lift the heavy bolt that Cal had dropped to secure the door, but I couldn't get it to budge.

"I couldn't move that other one," he told me, handing me the hammer. "Hit hard with this, hit up."

As I braced myself, and began to hammer at the bolt, I heard him turn to Pat.

"Try the house," he told her. "There ought to be a phone somewhere out here in the stable, but there has to be one in the house. Call the fire house. Call the police."

We couldn't make each other hear without shouting. The flames had snaked their way across the grass to set one of those big trees along the circle drive on fire. It blazed like a giant torch against the sky. The noise was deafening. Only once in a while could you hear the desperate screeching of the peacocks over the crackling of the flames. And over it all, both Shadow and Stormy were leaping around barking alarms. The air was so hot that I felt as if my skin was burning.

When I got the heavy bolt knocked out of its slot, I tried the door handle. Not until it failed to turn in my hands did I remember the rattle of the key in the lock as Cal left. This was too much. I swung the hammer as hard as I could against the metal lock and it gave in a splintering of wood. I reached inside, turned the handle, and opened the door.

I guess Mr. Peacock was saved because there was no way for the smoke to get into the locked room. I stumbled over him on the floor, just inside the door. I shouted for Ben to help me. We had to lift him across the threshold and down a couple of steps to the cinder walk. As skinny as he was, he really weighed a whole lot.

Together we dragged him outside, where it was light from the flames of the fire. I was right about Cal knocking him out. A stain of dried blood had darkened his white hair, right above his temple on the left side. I was sure glad I was wrong about him being dead. But even though he was still breathing, it was scary how pale and helpless he looked, lying there with tiny blue lines where his veins ran under his skin. He stirred, and seemed to gain strength in the outside air. He even groaned, and struggled with Ben and me a little as we tried to get him over on the grass where none of the burning wood would fall on him.

The minute we had him down, Ben was back inside that room like a shot.

"Oh, no," I heard him cry from inside. Then he was at the door, holding up a telephone with its cut cord dangling down his side.

Cal had thought of everything.

Ben shrugged, tossed the phone back into the room, and grabbed my arm. "Come on," he said. "Where did you say the woman was?"

Pat was coming around the house, yelling at us. "Locked," she called. "I've tried every single window and door I can reach. Everything is locked up tight."

As we always have, Ben and I read each other's mind just by looking at each other. "We could break a window and get in," I said. "But the chances are that phone is wrecked, too. You must have ridden Tony."

"Tony," Ben was saying in the same breath.

Then he was off and running toward the lower part of the lawn. "Keep trying!" he yelled back at us. "I'll get help!"

Pat was staring at me. "We have to break in," I told her. "It could take him longer than he thinks."

Ben was on Tony's back, galloping toward the gate, when I came back with the hammer I had used on the stable door.

"Listen," Pat said. "Listen to that."

Over the racket of the flames and the crackling wood came a high, shrill whine.

A siren.

I guess I have never heard a more beautiful sound in my whole, entire life. That siren rising and falling made my skin come up in little bumps all over my body. That time I didn't even pretend it was the smoke in my eyes that made them run, I just plain cried.

Help was coming. Help was really coming. Maybe it was the sheriff, maybe the fire engine. It didn't matter. Whoever was whining that siren toward the Peacock Place would break into the house, locked or not.

Pat had heard it, too. She grabbed me by the shoulders and held me very hard, her eyes streaming tears.

It wasn't one or the other; it was everybody. The sheriff's car pulled in first. He whipped that cruiser up the driveway, and then backed off onto the grass. He braked it to a stop well past where the wind was spreading the fire.

Right on his tail came the hook and ladder fire engine, with the fire marshall's red car right behind that.

Sheriff Higher was across the lawn faster than I knew he could move. He started to yell something, then stopped in his tracks at the sight of Mr. Peacock lying there in the grass with the dried blood staining his head.

"Miss Peacock's still in the house," I told him. "Somebody's got to break in to her. She's trapped up there."

He stared at me only a split second before shouting something to the men on the fire truck.

Then he turned away, walked briskly to his car, and started barking orders at his car radio.

All my life I had wanted to be right where the action was in a big fire — that shows you how much I knew. Believe me, once is plenty. Even with the best of help, which we seemed to have, a fire like that is pure horror, blazing heat, and flames leaping out of control, and always the rising sound of crackling destruction.

The firemen rolled out of that truck like bees out of a turned-over hive. Some of them started assembling equipment, while others attached the huge rubber hoses to the water outlet by the stable.

The first man off the truck, his face hidden by an immense hat, took the porch stairs two at a time and started hacking away at the big yellow door with an immense ax.

Within seconds, streams of water bathed the side of the house, pouring like waterfalls over the windows to run through the burned-out bushes, and along the blackened lawn. A new sound was added to that din, the angry hiss of fire being stopped by water.

Two of the posts that supported the roof of the stable had burned through, so that the roof leaned at a dangerous angle by the room where I had been trapped.

Pat stood shivering beside me, her arms tight

around my shoulders. Within minutes, another fire engine roared up the drive, with an emergency ambulance behind it. I felt my eyes still swimming with tears when two men in white leaped out and ran toward Mr. Peacock. Almost at once, they had him onto the stretcher, and into the back of the ambulance.

"Hobie, Hobie," Pat kept saying in this sick, numb voice. "What about Miss Peacock? Will she be all right?" For once, Shadow even had had more excitement than he could manage. He sat by my side, trembling, with his head pressed hard against my leg. I only knew that Ben had come back when Stormy joined us, whimpering a little as he collapsed at Pat's side.

"I met the sheriff down the road," Ben told us. "Is somebody taking care of that old man?"

I nodded, unable even to answer him. There was more going on than I could follow. A man came to the front door of the house and called to the ambulance crew. A paramedic was there at once, following him back into the house.

"I started this fire," I told Pat. "I was trying to signal for help and I started this fire."

She and Ben both looked at me, but neither of them said a word. I felt like turning and walking away. Not really. I felt like turning and running away, and never having to face Sheriff Higher, or Miss Peacock, whom I could have burned alive,

112

or my folks, who would have to come home and hear about all this.

"We would have died," I went on. "All three of us would have died if you hadn't come."

It only struck me then that I didn't even know what had brought Ben and Pat out there, but there was no time to ask. The sheriff, who had gone in with the fireman, came to the door and shouted.

"Okay, Hobie," he shouted at me. "Get yourself in here. Miss Peacock wants to talk to you."

The hoses were still streaming water on the side of the house, and the stable, and the high branches of the trees. The peacocks were still screaming hoarsely from out back, and the hoses hissed and gurgled, but there weren't any flames anymore. One side of the beautiful yellow house was charred and ruined. The bushes and trees were dried black skeletons against the lights from the trucks and cars.

Shadow's cold nose kept shoving into my fist, but I couldn't take him along. I remembered the sheriff's anger right after the parade. This wasn't anything I could blame on Shadow, or anyone else.

I could feel how much Pat wanted to come with me, but I turned and shook my head.

"Just keep Shadow," I said, starting toward the drenched and shattered front door where Sheriff Higher was waiting.

Unopened Mail

I had been having my problems with Sheriff Higher for years, but he had never looked as scary before as he did waiting there in the hall. His face was all red and puffy, as if he had been running too fast and too far. His mouth was drawn tight in a line, like a man trying to hold words back.

A single lamp with a crystal shade spread a fan of light on the curving stairway that came down into the hall. Rooms opened off on both sides, with only looming shapes of furniture visible in the darkness. The floor of the hall glistened wetly from the water that had poured in when the door was broken down. A lot of blue glass was scattered across the floor, with peacock tail feathers in among the shards. I guess there had been a big vase of them sitting at the bottom of the stairs.

The sheriff didn't speak to me again. He simply turned and started up the stairs ahead of me, his boots loud on the polished floor.

Miss Peacock was standing by the window with

her back to us, leaning a little to the left on the ivory cane. As she turned, I thought that even though she was hardly tall enough to be a full-grown woman, she had a royal look like Caliph Haroun had, something in the way she held her head under that crown of soft white hair.

She just looked at me a long minute and then smiled.

"They tell me your name is Hobart Morgan."

I nodded. "Yes, ma'am."

"And your dog is called Shadow?"

I nodded again.

She held out her hand to me and I stepped forward, conscious of the sheriff silent beside me.

"Tell me what you know about all this," she ordered. Her hand really felt strange, not warm and moist like Pat's had out there in the yard, but cool and dry, as if it was just skin and bones with no fat at all in between.

I didn't know where to start and glanced over at the sheriff.

"Miss Peacock told me about your coming in to get your dog," the sheriff said, as if the words were pretty hard to get out. "What do you know about this Calvin Prentice?"

I stared at him. How did he know Cal's whole name like that?

"There was a plot," I began. "Mr. Peacock made it. He told this Cal —"

Miss Peacock's hand tightened on mine. "Mr. Peacock?" she asked. "My brother?"

Suddenly she didn't seem to feel like standing up anymore. Sheriff Higher was there in a second, helping her back into the big, blue wing chair. Only then did I see the ropes, loose around the chair, as if someone had been tied into it.

That was why I hadn't seen her again. That was what Cal had meant when he said he fixed her so she wouldn't get in his way. But she had worked her way free, even as I did. She had worked her way free, and watched me set that fire from her window.

"The man with the white hair," Sheriff Higher said. "He is the real Mr. Peacock, then?"

I nodded. "Cal knocked him out, and left me tied up in the tack room."

"My brother," Miss Peacock broke in. "He's here? Where is he? I have to see him." Her voice had turned all urgent and fluttery.

The sheriff looked doubtful. "He's outside with the medics. I could see what they say."

"Do," she said. "Oh, please do."

"The whole plot was his," I blurted out. "He and Cal were taking the horses to sell them. Then Cal double-crossed him and knocked him out."

"Wait, wait," Sheriff Higher said. "Let me check on Peacock." He paused at the door and looked at

Miss Peacock. "Could you come downstairs if they could bring him in?"

She nodded. "I'm only a little stiff. Hobart will help me."

She held the bannister with one hand, and I held her other arm. She had just flicked the lights on in the room to the left of the front door when the two medics brought Mr. Peacock in, walking a little unsteadily between them. He had a thick, square bandage on one temple, and his eyes looked sick.

"You fellows wait outside," Sheriff Higher told the men from the ambulance. "We won't be long."

They had helped him into a little divan kind of thing with a curved back. Miss Peacock was there beside him in a minute, her hand on his arm.

"Madison," she said gently. "You're here, you're really here."

He shook his head. "Don't, Phemie," he said. "Don't be kind to me. I've done a terrible thing to you, and I can't stand your being kind to me." He had pulled his arm away from her touch, and wouldn't look at her. Instead, he looked off to the corner of the room like a whipped animal.

"I want to understand this," she said. "Why didn't you write? Why didn't you call?"

He stared at her. "Write? Call? I've done nothing else for five years. Every letter came back marked no, and they hadn't even been read. Every time I called, I got Anderson, who said you were taking no messages."

"I didn't mean from you," she gasped.

He shook his head. "I had reverses. I was deeply in debt, and desperate. At first I only thought I could borrow money from you. Then my attorney read Father's will that gives you the house and grounds, and half of the income from the stables. There was money here for me, but I couldn't get to it. I even started legal action to declare you incompetent, to try to reach some of my assets."

She shook her head in disbelief. "But Madison, I never meant. . . ."

"You had built this wall around yourself so that you couldn't even be reached. The hedge, the locked gate, those screaming birds of yours, and Anderson keeping everyone at arm's length. What could I do?"

"What did you do?" Sheriff Higher asked firmly.

Mr. Peacock's hand strayed to his bandage, and he sighed. "I decided to take enough of our property to get myself back on my feet, even if I had to steal it. I met Cal in Hong Kong, and he agreed to work with me. When we found a buyer for the horses, I wrote to Anderson myself. I told him I was coming home for the winter, and would take over his management here. I told him I wanted to surprise Phemie here. I sent him the last money

118

I had to take a long, much-needed vacation."

"He just left. He never explained a thing," Miss Peacock said. "One day he was here, and the next day there was only that dreadful man with the snake on his arm."

Her brother flushed. "I can never forgive myself. But Anderson never saw Cal, he only saw me. He recognized me and went off thinking you were in for a great surprise."

"The word went around town that you were traveling with Anderson to South Carolina," Sheriff Higher told her. "That was why I didn't pay any attention to Hobie's story about your breaking the window and all."

"I had that story put out," Mr. Peacock said dully. "Like Cal said, I planned too well. We had given all the regular stable help paid holidays, and shipped the rest of the horses on ahead. Caliph Haroun would have been gone, too, except that Anderson made such a point of his being expected to lead off the Homecoming Parade." He sighed again, looking down at his hands. "So they are gone, Phemie. They are all gone. They will be out of the country now, shipped beyond recall. The time schedule was that tight."

"All but Caliph Haroun, maybe," Sheriff Higher said.

We all stared at him. He ducked his head and nodded. "Hobie put more doubt in my mind than he knew he did. He pointed out that the man who represented himself as Mr. Peacock was a lot younger and meaner than he should be. I agreed with him enough to send out a description to other law enforcement agencies. It took a while, even with that cobra tattoo on his arm. In the meantime, I kept an eye on the place, cruised out here every hour."

I groaned. "That's why I made the big mistake with the fire." He studied me, frowning as I explained about the torch and waiting for him to come at midnight. He was nodding by the time I was through.

"That was a freak of timing, Hobie. I was on my way out here at a quarter to twelve, when the report came in on this Calvin Prentice. He was wanted for grand theft. Before I could catch my breath, one of the deputies reported seeing the Peacock van going south on the state highway, just inside the county line. I called for help, and went down myself to close in on him."

"You caught him?" Mr. Peacock asked, his eyes suddenly bright in that pale face.

"We sure did," the sheriff nodded. "We got the whole kebash down at the jail — this henchman of yours, the van, and one restless Arabian horse."

I might have shouted if the fire chief hadn't appeared at the door.

"It's under control out there," he told the sheriff. "I'm leaving a couple of men with hoses in case of outbreaks, but the rest of us are heading back to town." He glanced at Mr. Peacock. "What about him? The fellows are getting restless."

"He can stay here," Miss Peacock put in swiftly.

"No, ma'am," the sheriff said.

"But I have no intention of pressing charges."

The sheriff nodded. "He still needs a thorough medical checkup, and probably some time in bed. He got a concussion, you remember." The sheriff signaled me to walk out with him.

"I figured those two could use a few minutes together before they take him away," he said. "What about your sister and Ben out there? Do you think you kids could watch over Miss Peacock for a few hours? Her neighbors down the road, the Zimmermans, who put in the fire alarm, plan to come by in the morning. But I don't think she ought to be left alone here after all she's been through."

"That's fine with me," I told him. "But what about Mrs. Kelley?"

"I already radioed one of the deputies to go over and tell her you kids were all right, and helping me out." He grinned. "She'll do a lot of fretting and wondering, but nobody ever died of curiosity yet." He paused. "Although I will say this for you, Hobie Morgan: You came as close as anybody I ever knew."

121

Beyond the Hedge

Pat hadn't been the least bit self-conscious about her funny outfit, until she stood in the light in Miss Peacock's living room. Then, looking down at herself, she gasped, and blushed almost as red as my hair.

Miss Peacock laughed merrily. "Who knows, my dear? Has anyone set down a rule for the proper clothing to wear on a rescue mission? It might just be a puffy jacket, and jeans with a lavender top." Then she frowned. "My goodness, that top is rather dressy, isn't it? All that lace and ruffles, almost like a party dress."

"It is a party dress," Pat told her. "My best one. I got it especially to wear to the Homecoming Dance."

"She has fingernail polish to match it," I told her.

Miss Peacock stared at me, then took Pat's hand and examined her fingernails. "Delightful," she said, smiling. Then she looked up into Pat's face.

"Isn't it fun to match things up, and dress in pretty colors?" Her tone turned wistful. "I used to love doing that. I had the fans designed for the saddles, you know, and chose the colors myself."

Pat was glowing under this approval. I had always thought of her fooling with clothes and things as something sort of strange. I couldn't remember ever hearing anyone come out and approve of it the way Miss Peacock did.

Ben had leaned over to look at Pat's fingernails, too. "Neat," he said. "But she always looks neat, Pat does."

Then it struck me. "Ben," I said. "You came over on your horse Tony. How did Pat get here?"

Pat giggled. "Why do you think I pulled on jeans under my dress? I rode behind him. It was, . . ." she hesitated, and grinned at Ben, "not bad at all."

"Hobart," Miss Peacock said. "It strikes me that we have no idea what was going on while we were tied up here. Or is this making more sense to you than it is to me?"

I shook my head. "Somewhere along there I guess I gave up understanding what was going on," I admitted.

"Then you're hungry," she decided aloud. "Whenever I have trouble thinking things through I go fix a bite to eat, and right away my head works better."

"It's almost four in the morning," Ben told her, his voice doubtful.

"Four in the morning," she cried, her eyes wide. Then she rammed the ivory cane into the rug, and pulled herself to her feet. "No wonder Hobart can't think. No wonder I'm hungry. People who stay up all night always get hungry. Come along, let's see what that dreadful man left in my kitchen."

Shadow and Stormy, who had come in with Ben, lay under the table and watched Miss Peacock eagerly. "There's ham," she said, peering into the refrigerator. "All that man brought me three times a day were dry ham sandwiches. We sure don't want any more of that. Come and see, Patricia, what looks good, and easy to fix."

"I'm lost in the kitchen," Pat confessed. "Our mom is a super cook, and I do the dishes. Hobie knows a lot more about cooking than I do. He really watches how Mom does things."

She turned and stared at me. "Aha, a chef in the making. Then you come look."

Later when Pat told Mom about it, Mom kidded me about showing off. I didn't care. I was lucky to remember that cheese and egg dish Mom sometimes makes for Sunday breakfast. You could sure see why the Peacock stable runs so well: Miss Peacock is a natural boss. She had everyone working right off. She told Pat and Ben where to find everything they needed to set the table, and they did that.

I don't know how any dish that is so easy to fix can taste so good, but it was wonderful. I grated a layer of cheddar cheese into a flat pan and broke eggs on it, two for each of us. Then I mixed half and half with salt and pepper and some of that dry mustard from the yellow can, and poured it into the pan. While the cheese melted and the eggs baked, Ben made stacks of hot, buttered toast. By the time Miss Peacock set out three kinds of jam, Pat had thawed frozen orange juice, and poured big glasses for everyone.

While we ate, Pat and Ben told us about their evening. "I had just come in from the dance when Mom and Dad called from Springfield. They had this wonderful news that they had found a house for us where we could keep Shadow."

She had to stop and explain to Miss Peacock about Dad's new job, and our moving away. Miss Peacock looked a little downcast at that as Ben picked up the story.

"Since Pat wanted Hobie to have the good news right off, she called out at my house, thinking Hobie was spending the night there. It scared us both when we realized that nobody knew where he was. Their sitter, Mrs. Kelley, was already in bed asleep and my folks were, too."

"That's when I thought about this place," Pat said. "I remembered how worried Hobie was about the woman at the window. It was Ben's idea for us to ride out here and check. I didn't even take time to change, I just put on my jacket and jeans for the horse."

"You don't like horses?" Miss Peacock asked.

Pat hesitated. "Hobie and I have never known a horse who liked us. That makes a difference."

"I didn't realize Stormy was following, until I was halfway to get Pat. After that, we figured Shadow might as well come along, too. I'm sure glad we did. Shadow went running toward that tack room like he knew Hobie was locked up in there."

Miss Peacock shook her head. "I was almost sorry I had worked my way out of my ropes because I had to watch that fire go. I thought for sure that both my young rescuer and I would never see another morning come."

"It was really mean of that man to tie you up, then go off and leave you like that," Pat said.

Miss Peacock grinned and spread more blueberry jam on her toast, really thick. "I asked for it, Patricia. I did everything I could to signal for help. I tried the phone, and he had to pull that out. I hit the window with my cane to get Hobart's attention out in the yard. He was right with me, and jerked me back so fast that my head spun."

My eyes met Pat's. So that was why it had looked as if she disappeared. "Then I tried to signal Hobart the next afternoon, and he saw me. After the sheriff and Hobart left, he came and tied me up."

"Your brother must have kept out of sight pretty well for you never to have seen him," Ben said thoughtfully.

She nodded. "Poor Madison. I have driven him to all this terrible plotting, and now he is hurt."

"But he even tried to put you away for being crazy," I reminded her.

"Don't be harsh on him, Hobart," she said. "I've thought about what he said in the other room. Madison was out East, and I was here alone. I had a fall from a horse and being lamed made me a coward. I was afraid of people breaking in, and my not being able to protect myself. That's why I had that big, thorny hedge planted. That's why I started raising peacocks. They are better than any alarm system at giving warning."

"The people in town thought you were snobbish, and hated them. You even sent their letters back unopened."

I thought for a minute she was going to cry.

"See how easy it is for people to misunderstand one another? I was really afraid. Having Mr. Anderson do the mail was just another way of keeping the world away from me, and threatening me. Why shouldn't Madison think I was crazy? You have to be a little bit crazy to think you can wall yourself away from the world, and make anything but a prison for yourself. Anything that doesn't grow and change is dying."

Dawn had begun to come while we sat there eating and talking. I was sleepy, but not in a dazed, heavy way. I felt really excited to have gone through that long night like that, and still be there with Miss Peacock and Ben and Pat.

"You still haven't told me what you were doing the day you came running in here with Shadow," she told me.

When I told her about biking in the preserve, she shook her head. "That place used to be beautiful and I haven't even seen it since the hedge grew up."

"It's still really nice," Ben said. "I used to go biking there with Hobie until I got so wrapped up in my horse and the posse that I quit doing anything else."

"Not a good idea, Benjamin," she told him. Then she smiled. "How about a walk out there now. Is anybody game?"

Pat hesitated and looked at Ben. "Why don't you and Hobie go, while Ben and I clean up this mess? We had our exercise, if you remember."

Once we were outside, Miss Peacock turned and smiled at me. "Cooks should never have to clean up after themselves, don't you agree?"

Her rings clicked as she grasped the peacock fan on the head of her ivory cane. I started to help her on the rough part of the cinder walk, but she shook her head. "I've got to start branching out, doing more on my own."

When she smiled there in that soft dawn light she didn't look like any seventy-year-old woman. She looked more like a mischievous girl gone white-haired and wrinkled.

She moved slowly because of her lamed leg, and only once in a while did she put her hand lightly on my arm. She walked me around in back of the stable, and through a gate I hadn't known was there, buried in the hedge like it was. I opened it, and held the branches back so she could go through.

I wished it was spring in the meadow, because in April it is all downy with wild violets before the grass starts to grow. Or even summer would have been nice, because then the blue flax floats like a haze above the grass. Instead, the sky was a pewter color with the dead pasture grass a dull gold in the first light of dawn. The sun wasn't even coming up, but was just an apricot slit between two lines of heavy clouds.

She didn't seem to care. She stood and looked as if her eyes had been empty and needed filling up. Neither of us said anything, but her cheeks got shiny, as if she was crying silent tears that she didn't even bother to wipe off.

Then the peacocks began to holler beyond the fence, and she took my arm. "That will be the sheriff coming back to take you children home. What a wonderful night this turned out to be, Hobart."

I only nodded, because I knew I didn't have to say anything. It was funny that I already felt with her like I did with Ben, that she knew what I was thinking without a lot of words.

Footnote

By the time Sheriff Higher delivered Pat and me back home that morning I was way past even caring about the way Mrs. Kelley fussed over me. I had stayed up all night once before, when I was spending the night with Ben and we did it on a dare. Another time I scared myself so bad with a late, late movie that every time I started to drift off I heard something slithering in around the glass on my window.

This was different. I felt as if I had gained about forty pounds in each of my legs, and my tongue felt thick. My eyes still hurt enough from the smoke, that the last thing I wanted to do was keep them open.

Mrs. Kelley made us cinnamon toast and hot cocoa. I didn't even care that she made the cinnamon toast wrong. Mom toasts it on both sides and then butters it, before sprinkling on the cinnamon sugar and putting it in under the broiler. When you make it that way, the top is like cinnamon candy, and the toast underneath is really crisp. Mrs. Kelley just made buttered toast, and dusted the cinnamon sugar on it. It was gritty, and not very sweet, but I ate it anyway. I swallowed the marshmallow off my cocoa in one gulp, and was asleep before Mrs. Kelley finished pulling down my window shades and tiptoed out of the room.

Mom and Dad got in some time late that afternoon. They had been there for quite a while before their voices from the other room woke me up. Usually I don't like it when Mom grabs me and hugs me a lot in front of everybody. I must have been too dopey from the long nap to care, because it felt pretty good that day.

She kept running her hand along the side of my face as if she were pushing my hair back. That's what she does when she's been worried, and is glad that things have worked out all right.

"It's about time you crawled out of the sack," Dad kidded me. "Your grateful friend called, and she wants us to come out so she can meet the parents of her hero."

"Miss Peacock?" I asked.

Dad looked at me and grinned. "Saved anyone else's life lately?"

"How about Ben and Pat?" I asked. "It still scares me to think what would have happened if they hadn't come out there."

"That kind of talk I can do without," Mom said, shivering a little. She rose and called Pat out of her room. "Let's run on out there so Dad can start back to Springfield before it's too late."

Pat looked really beautiful. She had on a yellow T-shirt with a darkish stripe across it. Some of the color from the shirt seemed to glow in her face. She sure didn't look like the Pat who had stood out there crying with me at Peacock's the night before. We sat in the backseat, and I guess I was staring at her.

"Is something wrong?" she asked, frowning a little and looking down at her clothes.

I shook my head. "You look great. And I like the color your eyelids are today."

She looked at me, and bristled a little as if she thought I was making fun of her.

"I'm serious," I told her. "Everything always goes together. I really like that."

She smiled and looked the other way out the window. "Marmalade Gold," she whispered real softly. Then she held up her hand, so I could see that she had painted her fingernails the same color.

"Neat," I said. That sounded good, too. I started to ask her the name of that purple color she had worn for the parade, but Dad was turning in at the Peacock Place and I had to get out to open the gate.

There were cars all around. I recognized Ben's

father's car, with the sheriff's car parked right behind it. It made me sick to look at the place. All the bushes were gone from the one side of the house, and the stables were blackened. Somebody had set poles along to prop up the roof of the stable where it was sagging down there by the tack room. There were burned streaks all up the side of the house, with the paint rough-looking and bubbled. The branches of the one big tree looked like giant claws against the sky.

Mrs. Zimmerman, from church, opened the door to Dad's ring.

"Good to see you," Dad told her.

"Nice to be here," she said.

"I heard you folks turned in the alarm last night," Dad said. "We are sure glad you saw the fire."

She nodded. "We were still settling down after going to that great Homecoming Dance. But we watch for smoke anyway. Neighbors do that."

Miss Peacock rose by her chair when we came in. Her face had lost that gray look, as if she might have had a big nap, too. She put her hand on my shoulder the way she had at dawn and grinned at me. "Where's my friend Shadow?"

"We left that scamp at home," Dad told her, taking her hand.

"That scamp is always welcome here, as Hobart is," she added. I saw Ben's eyebrows shoot up and down at that "Hobart," and I made a face at him.

Mrs. Zimmerman served a cake she had brought from home. It didn't taste like a box cake. In fact, it tasted like a good, heavy homemade cake with lemon juice mixed into the batter, and lots of ground-up lemon peel both inside and in the frosting. From the way Mom tasted hers and then looked at it, I knew she would be asking for that recipe.

"I was just too excited to settle down today," Miss Peacock said. "I hoped my brother might be here to meet you all, too, but the doctor wants to keep him in the hospital for a couple of days. He has a concussion and he's not young, you know."

"But he'll be all right?" Pat asked.

"He'll be fine," she nodded. "And he might even be staying here with me. We talked about it when Mrs. Zimmerman took me to see him late this morning. We both feel that family should be closer than we've been. He'll be home here in just a few days." She turned to Mom and Dad. "I have something I want to give Hobart, but I felt that I should have your permission first."

Before they could answer, she nodded again and went on. "I want him to have one of Caliph Haroun's foals. They are fine Arabians, and he should have one for his own."

Ben's eyes went round as dollars, and he whistled under his breath the way he does. "But Hobie doesn't like horses," Ben said. He glanced at me, and I thought for a minute he was going to say I was afraid of them. I shouldn't have worried. "He thinks they're too big."

Miss Peacock laughed. "They are too big," she agreed. "They took some getting used to when I was growing up. But he would get this animal as a colt and could get used to it as it grows up."

I guess I just sat there stunned. I was thinking about Caliph Haroun, and the way his coat shone in the light. I remembered the wise way he had studied Cal, and had known that he had no business being put back in that van and hauled away. At the thought of owning a horse like that, I went all weak and funny inside. Miss Peacock was still talking.

"Sheriff Higher and I were talking this morning. He told me that even though Hobart was moving away, he was going to make him an honorary member of the Junior Posse, horse or no horse. The whole idea behind forming that posse was to make young people feel a part of keeping the law. Hobart certainly went out of his way, against odds, to help me."

I heard Ben's soft whistle again and looked over at him. He had missed me as much as I had missed him. He couldn't have been more excited if he were getting an Arabian horse himself. And he had a place to keep it.

A place to keep it.

I felt myself collapse inside. I had to get it said before this went any further.

"Gee, thanks so much, Miss Peacock," I said. "I'd rather have one of Caliph Haroun's colts than anything in the world. But you see, Dad had a hard enough time finding a place that would take Shadow. There's no way we could ever rent a house that would let us have a horse."

Everybody was looking at me in the funniest way. Then Dad grinned. "Didn't Pat ever get a chance to tell you the big news that made her call up Ben last night?"

"She told me you had rented a house," I said. I looked at Pat. She was grinning, too, with her shoulders pulled up the way she does when she is almost too happy to stand it.

"She said we could have Shadow there," I went on, trying to remember.

"That's all that seemed important at the time," she told Dad, still grinning.

"Can I tell?" Ben asked, practically jumping out of his chair.

At Dad's nod, Ben exploded into words. "It's not just a house, it's acreage on the edge of town. Pat told me all about it on the way over last night. There's a pasture and fences, and a pond where we can skate when I visit. And a barn for a horse."

I stared at Dad in disbelief.

In that moment of quiet, a big racket started

outside. The peacocks that had settled down when we came into the house began to scream and screech, until you could hear it through the closed window. Mrs. Zimmerman was quick to the door. When she turned back she spoke to Miss Peacock.

"There's a little black dog here with hair in his face and the brightest eyes I've ever seen. Oops."

As she spoke, Shadow shot by her and came skittering through the hall on his toenails. After the barest glance around, he went straight to Miss Peacock's knee and leaned against it.

"That dog," Dad said.

"That dog was in at the beginning," Miss Peacock said. "Why shouldn't he be in at the end? We must have some little treat for him, too."

"He'd love that lemon cake," I told her. "He's used to real good food at our house."

Everybody laughed, including Sheriff Higher. And I was right, too. Miss Peacock fed Shadow a bite of cake, and I thought he would wag his tail off. Then she looked up and our eyes met. There were spots of color in her cheeks, and she was sitting there with friends and neighbors, and she had "family," as she called her brother, coming home in a few days.

I looked over to see Ben grinning at me. We both were thinking the same thing. "Not half bad. Really, not half bad."